SLICK

ALSO BY EDWARD HOWER

SLICK

EDWARD HOWER

Cayuga Lake Books

Cayuga Lake Books

Ithaca, NY

Slick
by Edward Hower

First Printing – October 2012
ISBN: 978-1-60047-773-7

Cover Art by Mary Michael Shelley. *Long Cloud Sky with Clouds*
Carved and painted folk art. www.maryshelleyfolkart.com

www.edwardhower.com

Printed in the U.S.A.

0   1   2   3   4   5   6   7   8   9   10   11   12

For

Jim McConkey

1

It's still dark as I slip out of the city. My eyes keep flicking the rear view mirror to check if another car's tailing me. Oncoming headlights scream past me like tracer bullets. Sometimes, though, in those peaceful moments when I'm in the only car on the road, I ride the long hum of my tires and fly into a dream I've been having for years—the hay barn, the farmhouse with its sagging side porch, and out on the grass, the family all waiting to welcome me back.

After several hours north, I turn off the highway and drive along country roads past the shapes of sleeping houses and yards. In my headlight beams I catch homey glimpses of flower gardens, picnic tables, birdbaths. The only home I've got right now is this Cadillac with its prehistoric fins and wrap-around windshield and cave-size trunk full of tools, books, a few clothes. It would've been too sad bringing anything more from my old life in the city, better to start my new one travelling light. Meanwhile, in this land between lives, I breathe in a dewy grass smell and all of a sudden I'm a kid sticking my head out the window of Mr. Vernon's old pickup as we go clattering down the road to his farm. Once, when he needed to ship some cows early, he fetched me before dawn and I saw the sun burn crazed streaky purple above the fields, heard the air exploding with a billion birds' cheep-chirping like it was their very first time—like it was mine—to watch a day break out. Today I've timed my trip so I can watch the sunrise again as I get close to the farm and, after a good visit, reach the Canadian border by nightfall.

The road into the Catskill Mountains keeps squeezing narrower. In a shadowy haze I coast through empty towns that hunch small around me. When I get nervous passing like a ghost through dead streets, I speak out the letter I wrote last week to Mr. Vernon, Laurie, and Dolores. Gradually the black drains out of the sky and a fiery glow singes the edges of waking clouds. Then slanted red sunstreaks fly out to splash the sides of barns and houses. I love the way the beams flow down the rounded mountainsides and light up cows, sheep, horses chomping their breakfasts in the meadows. Look, here's a river I used to pass, riding in Mr. Vernon's truck. That was eleven years ago, when I was 15, so I check my map to make sure I'm really coming closer to Oak Hollow. I leave the valley, follow the road up a long, long slope. Soon the asphalt turns to gravelly dirt with twisty trees crowding the shoulders.

Now I sense something's up ahead. It seems to be blowing a metallic chill into the air. I slow down, swerve around a sharp corner. And there it is, the state camp. Hell, I knew I'd have to pass the place but didn't expect it to loom up so fucking soon. There's the gnome-hatted guard tower and the chain-link fence with its metal posts standing in their cement boots. I skid to a halt. The Caddie growls.

I remember pressing my forehead into that fence, printing cross-hatched grooves in my skin as I stared *out* at the world through that goddamn wire. I ought to be laughing now, sitting pretty on this side of the fence, *in* the world and about to peel away with a spray of gravel. I'm free of this pen forever, aren't I? That's not quite how it feels. The camp gives off a cold magnetic force that makes my eyes ache and tugs with invisible hooks at my skin.

Surrounded by bristly forest, the low buildings squat on a dirt clearing as raw as an eczema sore on a porcupine's ass. The scrub trees I remember, they've grown into tall pines whose arms loom over everything, dripping long green sleeves. The buildings' roofs are soaked in shade. On the gate there's a metal sign—

N.Y. STATE POLICE TRAINING FACILITY AUTHORIZED PERSONNEL ONLY

Holy shit! This is no place for me to be hanging around! I duck down, squinting through the steering wheel like the fugitive I probably am. In the lot, half a dozen cop cars are parked, chrome teeth grinning in front and, above the row of blank windshields, cyclops top-lights instead of the blue flasher bars that cruisers have in the city. The buildings' windows are dark, it's too early in the morning for the "authorized personnel" to be here—but it won't be for long.

Most of the old structures have been torn down, replaced by shiny new cinderblock ones the color of frozen puke. But I'm not sure the new place is completely open for business yet. The old barracks—that grim kid-warehouse—is still standing. Look at the door, the slab of metal that the social workers locked and unlocked to regulate our lives night and day, it's hanging crooked from one of its hinges now. Just outside, metal bed frames are stacked like skeletons—our old double-bunks, scabbed with rust, stripped of mattresses.

Sometimes, when I shut my eyes tight, a movie-like scene flashes into the darkness behind my lids, and right now, in a split second, I see my Caddie smashing through the fence—the cop cars suddenly swarming at me in formation—rifles flashing out the windows—and down I go in a fire-storm of bullets. Blinking my eyes open fast, I grab the dashboard. But it's just quietly vibrating along with the engine's idle, motionless. The Caddie, my armored pal, wants to keep me safe.

I got to get out of here! *But where's the road to the farm?*

It used to curve along this fence into the forest, then wind through the dark trees and out into the valley. But all I see ahead of the car are brambles, rusty-looking sumac plants, monster weeds. Wiping sweat from my eyes, I check my new map. There's the thin black line I followed from the highway…but it just *stops* here at the camp instead of going into Oak Hollow!

I rip the map to shreds. I pound the steering wheel with both fists. Then I stop, ashamed, and clean all the scraps of paper from the floor, gently squeeze the leather wheel cover back into place. Sorry, sorry….

When I turn the key in the ignition, the engine rumbles, low and confident again. I drive at a creep through the tall scrub. Leaves scrape the fenders and claw at the wheels, but up ahead—yes! There's the back gate where Mr. Vernon used to pick me up for work. One last time I glance at the barracks where I first got to know him.

Late into the nights, we used to sit in ratty old armchairs at the end of the row of bunks. The barracks were nearly dark with only a line of yellow bulbs glowing like rodents' eyes along the ceiling. When I couldn't sleep, he'd let me stay up with him and we'd talk in low voices. Talk and talk.

The old man always had the midnight-to-eight-shift, he was the lowest grade of staff in the camp but to me he was the highest there was. His job was to just patrol the building to see that none of us junior felons broke out. Not real likely to happen—because most of the guys believed the social workers' bullshit about the camp being surrounded by a wilderness full of ferocious bears and black-bearded mountain men with shotguns lying in wait for escapees. And because we were too crapped out to go AWOL after chopping down trees in that wilderness, "conservation work," it was called.

Mr. Vernon was always exhausted, too, from having to do two jobs—the farm and the camp. He looked fierce with his craggy chin and eyebrows like white wires and deep lines in his cheeks. But I knew he was the opposite of fierce. He was the only staff who never hit kids or raised his voice at us. He'd tell me stories about when he was my age, how he'd learned to take care of animals, nail shingles on a barn roof, keep a tractor engine in running order—all the stuff he was gradually teaching me at his place.

The social workers were always pestering kids to tell them about our "home problems" and why we'd done our crimes, but I refused to open my trap to any of those bastards. Mr. Vernon never asked me a thing, though. He just let me talk if I felt like it. At two in the morning when everybody but me and him were asleep, with his spicy-smelling pipe smoke clouding around us—then I said things to him that I'd never told anybody. About my mother, all the foster homes the state sent me to, my runaways and busts, even the woman I almost killed. He never got disgusted with me or backed off. He listened.

I left the camp to work at his farm most late afternoons and weekends for the twelve months of my sentence. As he drove away from the gate, he'd tell me about the chores we needed to do that day. My muscles would start to tighten and twitch—like they're doing right now—because I was in such a rush to grab a hammer, yank open a barn door, get my hands around any job he had to give me.

The Caddie rolls forward through the high weeds. We rock and thump over invisible ridges, we crunch branches, shove giant leaves aside. Fuck the map—that road's got to be out there somewhere!

2

I can feel the car struggling, tires spinning in the dirt. It's a twenty-two-year-old 1960 Eldorado longing for straight city streets to drive on, not this backwoods no-man's-land. I grip the wheel tighter, lean forward…and there it is—a dirt track beyond some scraggly bushes! I press down on the accelerator.

Big mistake. *Whssssshhh!* A blast of mist shoots up from the hood. I switch off the engine fast. The geyser collapses. After a startled silence, a mob of bugs hisses all around me--laughing their tiny asses off while I sit here buried up to my hubcaps in underbrush.

"Shut up!"

They keep up their screeching. I drum my fingers on the wheel, breathe slower, slower, slower, and half-close my eyes. Just let the old Caddie cool down a while, like I need to do, too. With the engine off, I swear I can feel something throbbing behind me in the trunk. It's the cellophane-wrapped brick of cash that's been festering there for weeks. I still don't know what the hell to do about it. Maybe I should have left it in the city but somehow I couldn't--I just shoved it under the spare tire and piled my stuff on top of it. Never mind, I'll figure everything out once I get to the farm. My life was always a lot clearer there.

I remember the warm, piney scent of the forest as Mr. Vernon drove through it. Sunbeams flickered onto the road between the tree trunks. Then the truck picked up speed, bounced and rattled as it shot out of the woods, and we flew into open sky at the top of a long slope. Down we plunged into the sudden glare, the patchwork fields glowing all shades of green and gold below us.

The valley may have looked like the Promised Land, but Mr. Vernon said the countryside wasn't in such great shape. "Pete, family farms are going under 'cause most folks can't afford to work them any longer," he said. That was why he'd taken the night job at the camp, he needed the extra money to keep his place going.

Some of the old "dry walls" beside the roads had collapsed into long piles of stones. "They're over a hundred years old," he said. "Must've been an awful lot of work to build." Tell me about it! I used to break my back picking up rocks and lugging them to the fields' edges and finding places to fit them in, like I was one of the old-time pioneers. But Mr. Vernon paid me 50¢ an hour to work, which was a whole lot of money back then—we were only getting *50¢ a day* from the camp for chopping down trees.

Hell, I'd have fixed all Mr. Vernon's walls for nothing. It felt *clean* to be out in the green world, after suffocating in that gritty concrete camp. I loved walking over field after field in all kinds of weather, sunlight, drizzle, snowstorm, I didn't care. Having the run of the barns was great, saying Hello to the cows in their stalls, watching the way they gazed back at me with their sad bulgy eyes like they understood just how I felt, myself, being penned into a barracks every night. Mr. Vernon gave me a lame girl calf whose mother had died. He taught me how to feed her from a bottle and wash her down so her coat shone. I'd sit close against her in her stall, we'd keep each other warm when the snow blew across the barnyard. Finally Mr. Vernon and I helped her learn to use her legs to stand without falling over, and she joined the herd. Laurie and Dolores kept an eye on her for me while I was back at the camp.

I didn't even mind her trying to kick me when I walked too close to her hind legs. I felt like kicking somebody most of the time myself, crowded together with 59 other kids in that penal colony—like the Siberian ones I read books about, years later. No room to turn around in without shoving up against some asshole who'd gut-punch me for stepping onto his turf. What did I know about all that turf bullshit? I was raised in a dumpy old house in Yonkers with no drug dealer's territories for blocks away—the only kid in the camp who didn't come either from an inner city ghetto or some Appalachian shantytown. A misfit in a gulag of misfits.

When I first started working at the farm, I was too nervous around the family to come inside the house to eat with them, they had to feed me on the porch "like I was a pet," Dolores said. Country life spooked me in those early days. The girls used to grin when I first ran from a swooping bat or jumped away from a garter snake that flickered past my foot. Laurie grabbed the little snake and held it up to show it to me. The rippling of its tiny scales hypnotized me. I had to touch them, take the snake carefully from Laurie, let it slither through my palm. I could feel through my skin that it was getting scared, so I knelt down to let it slip

9

away in the grass. Pretty soon after that, when Mr. Vernon asked me again to join the family at the kitchen table, I came right in. And ate more than anybody, I couldn't help it—they kept passing big dishes of food to me every time my plate got empty.

I liked to help Laurie with the haying. Mown grass got raked in long rows by a tractor dragging wide prongs, then it was scooped up by a machine that spat bales out the back, all tied up with twine. I'd heave those big straw bundles onto the flat-bed truck that Laurie drove slowly around the field. If the skies frowned over with black clouds, I got to stay gathering bales before the rain could start, even after dark. The truck shot long luminous cones into the night and turned specks of dust to swirling sparks.

Laurie parked so that the beams lit the inside of the barn. She went in and stood on a low plank platform inside while I handed the bales up for her to stack. One night when we were both wobbly from exhaustion and heat, she turned her back on the tall pile she'd built. The bales started to totter over. I jumped onto the platform with my arms out to keep them from falling on her. Down they toppled—on me! The next thing I knew I was on my back under blocks of hay, gasping in the crushing darkness. I heard Laurie grunting somewhere, trying to dig me out. As I wriggled toward the sound, I felt her hand, grabbed it and heaved myself up. But when I tried to stand rubber-legged in the sudden fresh air, I pitched right into her. Down we went together, both tumbling over that straw mountain.

"You crazy bastard, you could've got us killed!" she wheezed at me.

"So could've you!" I coughed back. "You're supposed to be the fucking expert at this!"

She laughed. "Trying to be some big hero!"

"You owe me one, bitch!"

I didn't know much about talking to regular people when I started working on the farm, and was scared she'd be pissed off at me. But then I was sitting against a wall with her wiping the blood from my scraped cheek with the blue bandana she always wore around her neck. My skin stung from the sweaty cloth but I loved the feel of it.

I'm picturing Laurie now like she was still the same age she was eleven years ago, at twenty-five. She was a stocky, flush-faced girl. Her high, round cheekbones made hollows for her eyes. She'd give me blue twinkly looks that made me laugh, like she and me were in a secret conspiracy against all the hotshot bullshitters of the world. Her yellow hair was braided in a rope that danced against her back when she walked, her ass rolling in her jeans and her big grapefruits bouncing in the tie-die shirt she wore untucked and flapping in the breeze. That was 1971 when there were left-over hippies still around, I don't think people had heard the '60s were over up here in the boonies.

"Here you go, Slick," she'd say at the dinner table, filling my lemonade glass.

She called me that because once I bragged to her about how slick I was at boosting cars. When she asked me what offense I'd been sent to the state camp for, I told her straight out, "Grand theft auto." She asked me what kind of cars I liked, and I said Lincolns, because once I drove a Lincoln Continental around for, well, it was just half a day before I got busted. But I didn't cop to that, I just said I took it on a little trip which was like driving an ocean liner it was so quiet and powerful.

She said she liked Caddies, the old kind with fins from here to Texas. I think she said that to make Dolores smile. Dolores was from Texas, though she was born in Mexico. She lived with Laurie in one of the big old farmhouses on the land Mr. Vernon owned. He usually slept in the house a few miles away where he and his wife had lived before she'd died. At first he didn't seem to like Laurie having Dolores around but then after a while he did. Once he even said she was a good influence on Laurie, which made both girls laugh. I know they were grown women but everybody called them girls then, including them. Dolores was so polite with Mr. Vernon it was like she thought he was a priest or something.

There were times when he got on Laurie's case real bad. Once it was because she'd stuck a big round peace sign on the bumper of her pickup truck. He said it was disrespectful to her brother to drive around with that sticker. She snarled back that it would be disrespectful for her *not* to have one. She clenched her forehead tight, and her braid seemed to swing like she'd like to whip it across his face. But pretty soon she was laughing and kidding her old man out of his gloom.

Dolores stayed away from the fights Laurie had with her old man about Vietnam, they made her look sad and scared. But usually Dolores had a beautiful smile. Her lips spread wide, pushing round dimples up into her cheeks. I loved the gap between two of her top teeth, just off to the side, it made her look like she was hinting about something dark and secret. Her face was flatter than Laurie's, her skin golden, her eyes almost black, Indian-looking, or maybe Asian. She told me that kids in Mexico used to call her "China,"—"*Cheena,*" she said it—but she'd just toss her silky black pony-tail at them to make them smile and feel stupid. Her eyelashes reminded me of butterfly wings, I wanted to feel them fluttering against my fingers. She liked to call me Pedro.

Once in a while Dolores and Laurie called me String-bean, which I was in those days, at least when I first began working on the farm. My chest was scrawny, my cheeks were caved in and my nose poked out like it was always sniffing the air for predators. I kept my hair so short that Laurie said my head looked like a dandelion you could blow all the fuzz off. I didn't like looking fuzzy but I learned the hard way when I first got to camp that if I had long hair, some gangbanger would grab a handful and slam my head against a wall.

I liked the nicknames the girls called me, I'd never had any before. I could become a whole new guy when I was with them. I never gave them any names, their real ones were good enough for me. *Laurie'n'Dolores* The names sounded like a song. I could hum it over and over under my breath—even during times, years later, when my throat was clenched so tight I couldn't make any other sound.

The girls gave themselves nicknames, at least when they were doing their lunch business, driving to constructions sites around the county to feed the workers. They'd boil up Mexican food in big pots and make brownies on trays, then load them into Laurie's truck. Once I was cleaning out a barn and heard a lot of guys cheering down the hill, so I climbed into the rafters and peered through a hole in the wall to see what was going on.

Workers in yellow hard hats were gathering around the pickup, big grins on their faces. The girls stood on the cab roof. The men hushed, waiting, watching them. Then Laurie and Dolores belted out a song—

"I'm TA-CO!" Laurie sang.

"I'm EN-CHEE-LA-DA," Dolores sang.

And together—*"We hope you like the lunch we've brought today...."*

I forget the rest of the verse, it was dumb but that didn't matter, because when the girls finished, they made high-pitched *yip-yip-yip!* sounds and suddenly lifted up their t-shirts. Laurie bounced her pale grapefruits and Dolores bounced her golden peaches! Only for a few seconds, while they *yipped,* their nipples bobbing in the air. Then they yanked down their shirts and spread their arms high in the air like cheer-leaders. The guys *yip-yip-yipped* their heads off, a pack of happy coyotes. They couldn't get their wallets out fast enough to pay the girls for the lunches and the cans of cold beer.

There were two kinds of brownies for sale, one for a quarter, and another kind for a dollar, which seemed like a lot to me. Then one day I was driving back from haying in Laurie's truck, sitting squashed between her and Dolores, when we passed a garden mostly surrounded by bushes and a kind of fence made out of tarpaulin sheets held up by poles. I asked what was growing there, and Laurie laughed.

"You probably thought that stuff came in plastic baggies right from the factory," she said to me. She was driving with one hand on the wheel, the other hand dangling out the window and slapping the door in time to a country song from the radio. "Didn't you, Slick?"

"Baggies?" I was a little slow that day, worn out and high on the girls' delicious-smelling sweat I was soaking up in the cab.

"Welcome to the Garden of Eden, Pedro!" Dolores poked me softly in the ribs.

"Ohhh," I said, and grinned. I'd never seen marijuana growing before. I couldn't believe how tall the plants were, like secret green fountains gushing up out of the ground.

My grin fades as I sit here in my car. And for a moment, what I wish most is that the girls had never told me about that garden of theirs.

I twist the key in the ignition again. The engine idles clean and smooth. No radiator hiss, no steam. I shift into low gear, edge slowly forward. I plow on toward that dirt track. The Caddie lurches, and its tires find the road on their own, I swear. We roll along it, free of all the green gristle that's been holding us back.

Soon high pines surround me, casting so much shade that no more underbrush can grow. My engine purrs as I roll farther and farther into the forest. Gradually the sunbeams stop flickering, the shadows darken around me. The roof of branches overhead makes the darkness so deep that I have to switch on my high beams to keep from driving off the road. Even they don't reach far enough for me to see what's coming up.

3

I roll out of the woods blinking hard at a blast of light. The fields I've remembered being so luscious green and golden are still spread out before me in the valley below, and I coast slowly downhill. Ahead is a Y in the road. I remember it…but is the turn-off to the farm to the right or the left? *I don't know!* Shit!—how could I have forgotten the way? I'm so goddamn whacked with exhaustion—four weeks with hardly any sleep or food, wandering the pavements glancing over my shoulder, driving the night streets, grieving my heart out.

I wasn't supposed to make the drive through the night alone like this! My fiancée was going to be sitting in the seat beside me on this trip. Me and Raquel planned on heading to Montreal to start fresh, far from the people she said were closing in on her. Raquel always loved to hear me talk about my old days on the farm, and I couldn't wait to have her see the place, meet the family. They'd have loved her, they really would. Since her death I haven't been able to think straight about anything. Except coming back here….

My forehead rests on the steering wheel for a long time. Finally I sit up and wipe my eyes dry. Then I gun the engine and—guessing—swerve to the left. The Caddie and I plunge on down. It's a familiar feeling, this fast drop, it even feels good…but after a few moments I know it's not the way to the farm. I could brake, turn around, but to tell the truth, I need more time to get re-oriented up here in the country. I don't want Mr. Vernon, Laurie, and Dolores to see me acting like a zombie. Or looking all draggled and sweaty. My clothes are a mess, my hair matted all over my shoulders, the stink coming off me must be like a goddamn dumpster's. I hate to risk being seen, but I got to clean up somewhere—change my threads, get myself decent-looking for the family.

I glide on down, level off…and now I'm coming into Oak Hollow. Laurie wrote in one of her songs that it was "the little town that time forgot." At the end of the first verse she rhymed "forgot" with "beauty spot." But at the end of the last verse, the rhyme was "my brain cells rot."

I drive slowly toward the old white clapboard houses, and at a distance the town's as pretty as I remembered it— neat green front yards set back from the quiet road, all shaded by a long awning of tree branches. As I come closer, though, the buildings look worn out, their paint flaked, front porches sagging under some invisible weight.

I come to the two churches on either side of the old cemetery. One's got a fresh white paint job and a bronze plaque beside the door—This Edifice was Erected in 1801 for Sawmill Workers and Farmers…and so forth. Once I went inside and saw what Mr. Vernon said was the family pew, one of a couple dozen long gleaming benches. The air was sweet with the smell of flowers, it splashed up red and white from a huge brass bowl on the altar. Above it was a stained-glass window where a shepherd gazed at glowing gold mountains like the ones above the town at sunset. Over the years, I've seen these mountains in my dreams, but often in scorched black and white as if glimpsed in a lightning storm at night. It's good to see them in color.

Someone, maybe Laurie or Mr. Vernon, has mowed the church cemetery's grass. Older headstones poke up like mossy teeth. And look, there they are—the angels, just like I remember them! The same two stone ladies in curvy robes, still on duty on their pedestals! They face each other over some markerless plots, wings outstretched to comfort all the dead people, some of them probably here since 1801. They don't seem to have grown a bit older than they were when I last saw them. Man, does that cheer me up!

The ladies look like they never get to move an inch, year after year. Standing so still for more than a century must be hard work, especially in the winter with the snow piled up on their heads. You'd think they'd have to scratch an itch or go pee every now and then. Maybe late at night they rush off behind the church to do whatever it is angels do in off-hours. I hope they keep a bottle hidden back there so they can take a nip every decade or two, nothing too rowdy, just a clinking of silver cups in the moonlight before they whoosh out their wings and flap back to their perches.

I get out of the car, climb over the cemetery's low wall. "Hey, ladies! Remember me?"

Of course, Pete, one says, her voice whispery. *How could we forget?*

We always love visitors, the other ones whispers. *Especially you.*

I straighten my shoulders. "Hey, it's great to see you!"

You, too!

But you're looking like you just crawled out of a bombed building, or something worse.

What are you running from, Pete?

I frown. "You know, I'm not even sure."

What do you mean?

"I don't know if anybody's after me. Or how careful I got to be." It's scary as hell!"

You look like you're confused. Don't you think so? – she must be asking the other angel.

Who can't be nodding like that, can she? I rub my eyes hard.

Do you really think you can leave everything behind?

"Have to try," I say. "Or die trying."

What are you looking for back here?

"The farm. Mr. Vernon. Laurie and Dolores. Have you seen them?"

Of course.

"When?" I step forward. "Where?"

Silence.

"Hey, ladies—please!"

I wish we could help you.

But for us, minutes are the same as days, months the same as years.

So we couldn't tell you when we last saw them.

Or where. We don't get around much.

Silence. I ask them again, my voice cracking, but I don't hear anything but leaves rustling in some nearby trees. It's hard to read the angels' faces, the years have worn down their features so much. But I think I see shadows flicker across the nearer lady's lips. I take it for a smile, and walk on.

The newer section of the cemetery, behind a low wrought-iron fence, is where the modern graves are. I went there once with Mr. Vernon when he laid some flowers before the stone of his wife, who'd died exactly a year before, and on the grave of his son, Lance, who was killed in Vietnam just a few months after Mrs. Vernon passed. His jeep was blown up by a mine, he was thrown into a pond and drowned.

"A real hero, after all," Mr. Vernon said, kneeling there.

I had to help him to his feet, he was trembling so hard. I'm still choked up about it, even after all this time.

A pointed stone pillar stands on a mound of grass— the vets' memorial. An obelisk, Mr. Vernon called it. I imagined Lance leading a charge across enemy lines and rescuing wounded buddies in battle. I even dreamed about being buried near that pillar. When I was drafted to go to Vietnam, myself, I wrote my home address in my army papers as *c/o Vernon, Oak Hollow, N.Y.*, so they'd send my body back to this spot if I caught a bullet. Even now, I can't help picturing my flag-draped casket being lowered into the ground here, with Mr. Vernon, Laurie, and Dolores standing reverently by while some soldier boy in a white uniform blats out taps on a bugle, the slow notes soaring over the fields beyond the church steeple.

The bottom of the obelisk is drowned in the shadow of the other church. Its paint was peeling when I used to go by in the truck eleven years ago, and now the building's a total wreck, the siding wind-blasted down to a mean grey, the front wall looking about to collapse into kindling all over the road. On the notice board beside the door only a few wooden letters remain with gaps between. So whatever message the preacher—who's probably moldering under one of these stones—wanted to announce to his parishioners that final Sunday has turned to garbled vowels and consonants. The big round frame in front, where a window used to be, is empty except for the wires that held up the glass, and they're snaggled in a web for bats to fly into and get gobbled up by the giant spider that probably lives inside, playing a dead organ with its eight legs.

I pass a building that looks like the General Store / Post Office I remember, but there's no sign in the window. Seeing the store gives me a jolt, so I turn around and drive back to double-check. I've always remembered this place because it's where I met Laurie and Dolores on my first day in Oak Hollow.

Before I reached the camp, my social worker's car had engine trouble and sputtered up to the garage-barn behind this general store. While we waited for the mechanic to fix the engine, he let me walk around inside. Bastard warned me if I tried to shoplift I'd get a year added to my sentence. Not that there was much I wanted among the half-million things in that little place. The long shelves were packed, one sneeze and I'd have been buried in dog biscuits or canned peas or roofing nails.

A metal grate ran along the U. S. Post Office part of the counter, and next to an opening hung a framed certificate. *Emma D. Gaines is hereby appointed Postmistress of Oak Hollow, New York,* it read, *by Order of Woodrow Wilson, President.* It was dated 1913, and this was 1971, so Emma would have had to be around 100 or so, well maybe 80. I was figuring this when I saw a face with bulging eyes and deep creases running down the cheeks. It poked out of the grate's window like the head of an ancient turtle.

"Do you need any stamps, young man?" it croaked.

I jumped back, knocking axe-handles from a rack onto the plank floor. They rattled and rolled every which way like bones off a skeleton. My face flared red, because two girls had been watching me the whole time. One was light and one golden-skinned—Laurie and Dolores, though I didn't know who they were then. The pale one with the yellow braid strode over and started picking up the handles, so I did, too, though I worried that my worker would accuse me of trying to shop-lift axes or molest one of the town's young women.

As soon as I'd finished, I rushed up an aisle and stood in front of a shelf of little key chains, carved wooden animals, postcards. One of the souvenirs made my breath stop—a toy bark canoe. It was soft tan with rawhide sewn along the gunwales. My mom had given me one just like it for my birthday when I was little. She said she'd gotten it years earlier when she was a kid and she'd stayed in a big, white hotel in the mountains.

The place seemed like a magical castle to her—turrets and gables and verandahs, all surrounded by wide lawns, with a pond in back where swans paddled around. Its dining room floor shone like black ice, she said, and upstairs a maze of corridors led to big, high-ceilinged rooms. When she told me about the hotel her eyes sparkled, but sometimes she refused to talk about it when I asked her to, other times she even said she'd never even been there.

The canoe was the only thing of hers I'd ever seen from when she was my age, and I really loved it. First chance I got, I took it to the park and tried to float it in the little pond. But pretty soon it started to sink. I had to wade in to rescue it. The canoe wasn't made out of bark at all but some kind of cheap cardboard. It got so soggy that when I lifted it up, my fingers poked right through the bottom. I kept telling my mom how sorry I was and she kept saying how sorry *she* was, that nothing she tried to do for me ever worked out, and this was the story of her whole damned life. I dropped the wrecked canoe into the trash can. When the garbage truck came the next morning and I heard its motor grinding up everything, I wished I could get heaved into the truck's crusher jaws myself.

So seeing that canoe on the shelf in Oak Hollow didn't do much for my mood, which had already sunk lower than whale shit. Then I spotted some postcards on a rack. One showed a stream running through some autumn woods, **SOUVENIR OF THE CATSKILLS** it said in fancy lettering at the bottom. I thought of buying it, maybe mailing it to my mom. She was alive then, in a hospital in Nevada, though I doubt if she'd have recognized my name on a card, she was so far gone. But it didn't matter, I had no money. So I was putting the card back in the rack when the blonde girl stepped up beside me.

"You on your way to the state camp?" she asked in a brassy voice.

Now I saw that she was older than me, with crinkly smile lines at the corners of her eyes. I couldn't manage to speak, and just nodded.

"*Ohhhh,* boy!" The tone of her voice made me shudder, like she knew gruesome stuff about the place I'd be discovering soon enough. "You got a girl to write to?" She leaned over to look at the postcard I was holding.

Did I have a girl? I did til she vanished after my last court appearance. I didn't want to write her, or explain her to this pretty, round-faced stranger, either. So I said, "Sort of."

She nodded, then turned toward the turtle in her cage behind the counter. "Hey, Emma—put this card on my tab, will you!"

I was so speechless that I never got a chance to thank her. She and her friend walked out the door, and I thought I'd never see them again.

I step out of the car in front of the store. It looks like any big, two-story, country house now. I push my forehead against one of the window panes. Inside, the gray curtains are so wispy they seem about to dissolve into dust. The store looks empty, but I try to focus through the gauze anyway, searching hard for something. The canoe. For years after my first visit here, I dreamed about going back to buy it. And now I'm really here—but it's gone! *Shit!* I have to step back, catch my breath, walk around in circle. I feel like smashing a fist through the window but I shove my hands deep into my pockets.

I get back into the Caddie, my getaway tank, and drive toward the back of the store where the garage-barn used to be. Cars were parked outside the door with their hoods slanted up in the air like a row of open-mouthed hippos. Best of all, painted on the side of the barn was a winged horse that flew high in the air—like flying was just normal for horses, though it looked miraculous to me. God, what a beautiful sign!

And there's the barn! It's shut now, the big door padlocked, but right above it is the horse—still here! His eyes are fiery red, his mane's rippling backwards, his legs have just given a mighty kick, and he's off! He can fly wherever he wants, swooping and swerving around the clouds!

Maybe he dives down to the cemetery to visit the angels. They like to jump on his back to go for outings, since their own wings are cracked from being snowed on for so many winters. Away goes the horse with the angels on board, they soar up and up above the forest (and maybe he takes a dump onto the camp on his way over) and glide over the mountains north to a country where all the lakes are gleaming in the sun and the glaciers are rivers of diamonds.

4

I get up my nerve and drive about six miles from Oak Hollow until I find a truck stop where a clerk takes my $5 so I can get a hot shower and change my clothes. Scrubbed and shaved, probably smelling a lot better, I ought to feel great but for some reason I'm still nervous about seeing the Vernons. All of a sudden I'm hungry— for the first time since Raquel's funeral, I realize—and slow down as I pass a grocery store. A big black Crown Vic sedan's outside, so I park down the road and wait a few minutes, then drive back to see if it's gone. It is.

Beside the store there's a rusted trailer, its yard strewn with junk—a toppled washing machine with legs in the air, a rusty-toothed lawn-mower (where's the lawn?), amputee porch chairs (where's a porch?). A roped dog barks his lungs out at me, probably chomp my foot off at the ankle if I stepped too close. When I push open the store's door, dangling jingle-bells set up a frantic racket, a hillbilly burglar alarm. Hey—I'm a *customer*, for Chistsakes! Maybe I was better off when I couldn't feel hunger.

Passing a mirror under a Coca-Cola sign, I check my appearance. My hair's yanked back into an elastic band, my cheeks look caved in, and the skin around my eyes is bruised-looking. I put on my sunglasses, hope I look more normal. My jacket, $3.85 in a thrift store, is almost new. I bought it because it reminded me of the one my English prof wore, first teacher I ever saw in blue jeans and a sports jacket. My chest and shoulder muscles bulge it out too much, but it's still a good disguise.

A wrinkled troll steps behind the counter, lumpy in a gray Mother Hubbard dress. She squints at me as I find soda, bread, cans of baked beans, then take some orange cheese from a humming refrigerator. I need a knife to slice it, but the only kind the place sells is a hunting knife, which tells you something about the people that shop here. I picture a shack-dwelling hermit with a ragged beard and camouflage pants, he lives deep in the woods and roasts woodchucks over a campfire, using the knife's point to dig out charred guts and stuff them into his gullet.

I bring my stuff to the counter. "Hi," I say to the woman, like a normal person. "How're you doing?"

She peers hard at me. I take my wallet out to show her I'm no bum and pay with a fifty. When I see a cardboard display of corn-cob pipes, the kind Mr. Vernon used to smoke, I buy one and a can of his favorite tobacco, Prince Albert. She rings everything up. By now I'm used to her dismal face and feel like talking to her. It's been a month since I've spoken to anyone. Besides, I need information bad.

"Someone told me there was a man called Vernon, used to live around here, worked at that state camp." I say. "He had a daughter. Laurie, I think her name was."

The woman glares down at the counter. A fly buzzes against a window screen.

"Did you ever hear of them?"

Finally her mouth moves. "Maybe." Her voice is wheezy. "But I don't know nothing."

She's packing my stuff into a paper bag so fast she drops cans all over the counter. Suddenly I see my reflection in her glasses—a guy in dark shades and a sports jacket. I must look like an undercover cop to her! *Me!* I almost laugh out loud.

"Hey, lady, I'm just a guy!" I yank open my jacket. "Look! No badge, no gun! Okay?"

She looks up. "Didn't expect nobody asking about the camp, after all these years."

"I didn't mean to startle you. Sorry."

She nods, sighs. "Well…everybody knew the Vernons. Damn shame, it was."

"What was?"

"That riot. My nephew, John, he never got over it. He was a staff at the camp, too."

I almost say, "I remember him," but bite my tongue.

"You know what them kids done to John that night? They stuffed him in a locker. Wouldn't nobody let him out til the troopers got there. Must of been two-three hours."

I gape at her. *That* bastard was her *nephew?* "John" would have been John Murdock. "Murd," we called him, which a Cannuck kid told us was French for "shit." He was the fat creep who spat tobacco juice in my face on my first night when I refused to spread my cheeks so he could "check for contraband." My eyes burned so fierce from his squirt of brown spit that I thought I'd been blinded for life. During the riot, I saw him being squashed into that locker. The guys looked like they were about to snap his spine but I didn't give a rat's ass if they did.

28

I remember what Murdock did to scrawny little Fangs, a harmless psycho who'd been sentenced for stealing electronics from stores, he did it for a gang who told him they'd gang-rape his little sister if he didn't. He was called "Fangs" because he used to hiss and show his teeth like a rodent when somebody threatened him. Fangs got panicked if he wasn't dragging his fingers along a wall every second as he scuttled through the barracks. At wake-up one morning, when everyone was racing to the head bursting to piss, Murd parked himself against the wall, blocking Fang's way. Fangs didn't dare let go of the wall to move around him toward the toilets. Murd stood there grinning, a hulking no-neck porpoise in bib overalls. Piss streamed down the poor kid's legs, soaked his pajamas, trickling along the floor. Murd laughed like hell.

"Before the riot," the woman says, "people in town would knit scarves for those boys. Felt sorry for them, up here in the winter, so far from their homes and all."

"Scarves...." I remembered how warm they were. But I kept my mouth shut.

"John never could go back to the camp after that riot." She shakes her head. "When his mother died—my sister—he moved into my trailer. Seven years he stayed with me. My husband had passed and I didn't have no one to help me run the store. John did it all."

"What happened to Mr. Vernon?" I ask.

I'm not sure she hears me, she sniffles so hard. "I don't know how I'm going to keep this place going, now that he's gone."

"Who's gone?" I hear a crack in my voice. *"Who?"*

"John's gone! His heart. He had such a big heart, that boy." She turns her damp eyes up to me. "Not a boy—he was 59, just about to retire. One day he fell

down in a heap. Washing my breakfast dishes at the sink, and he just fell."

"That's…a shame."

She backs away from the counter. "I don't know why you want to come in here after all these years, asking questions," she wheezes. "There was a hearing about the riot. Investigators in suits talking to everybody in town that worked there. It was all settled at that hearing! None of those boys got seriously hurt—"

"Are you *kidding,* lady?" I lean forward. "Nobody *hurt?*—"

Suddenly her wheezes turn to barking coughs. I want to turn and run like hell but my feet seem nailed to the floor. She ducks through a door into a back room. The door creaks almost shut. I can feel her squinting at me out of the darkness. Man, have I fucked up!

On the counter are some bills and coins—the change she left me. I take another fifty out of my wallet and lay it down. Wrapping my arms around the paper bag, I rush away.

Back in Oak Hollow, I drive up the hill above the cemetery and swing onto a long narrow road, the one I didn't take before. I recognize the clackety-crunch of gravel under the tires. It always sounded like a drum-roll to me, still does, even louder. Mr. Vernon used to tell me that he'd never leave this land, it had been in his family for generations. He owned pastures of hay and alfalfa for the cows and horses, and on other hills, vegetable gardens and acres of corn. Laurie did half the plowing and milking and haying and keeping up repairs on the place. She'd once gone to Texas to agriculture college but came back after a year.

I can just see Laurie and Dolores running out of the house today in their jeans and flannel shirts. They'll hug me til I'm dizzy. Then they'll walk around the Caddie, peering into the windows, loving the way I've tricked it out inside with custom-tailored seat covers, wood grain trim, sculpted suede door inserts. Laurie will run her fingers along the beige leather seat-back and whistle. Great wheels, Slick! she'll say, Sure you aren't on the lam for this?

I'll grin and shake my head and tell Laurie, Hell, no, this beauty's legit! It only cost me three hundred bucks, took me a whole year to restore—engine, suspension, interior, everything. The scraped-down exterior looks like I've rammed it through a car wash that uses steel wool rollers-brushes. I'd planned to get it painted fire engine red, Raquel's favorite color, but I'm glad I didn't, I do not need to attract attention now.

Dolores will sit in the front seat, caressing the leather steering wheel cover, twirling the stereo dials. I can pick up city stations from here! She'll say, and bounce on the seat to a Latin beat, her pony tail flicking up and down. I'll lean in the window breathing the flowery scent of her hair.

The girls will look older, of course, but still they'll be in great shape from all the farm work. Hell, I'm older too, my hair's whitish gray even though I'm only twenty-six. Laurie and Dolores will go crazy that it's really me, back after all these years and looking so brawny and fit, too! Laurie will plant her hands on her hips, her braid swinging as she stares at my chest and shoulders. And look at Dolores smile! Mister America! she'll say. They'll bring me into the big parlor. It'll be pretty much like I remember, with the rocking chairs on the handmade spiral rug and the grandfather clock that was always bonging. It startled the shit out of me at first, I'd never heard one before. On the walls will be the Catskill landscape paintings that Dolores buys at flea markets—"Rip Van Winkle" was my favorite—and re-sells to antiques dealers. The girls' guitars will be leaning in a row along one wall, their curved bodies catching the light, gleaming.

There's Mr. Vernon. He'll look older, though he never looked young before, with his watery eyes and wrinkled cheeks. I guess his drinking didn't help his health, but who could blame him after what had happened in his family? Most adults made me nervous in those days, I knew they were going to try to make me feel weak and stupid so they'd have an easier time pushing me around. But the way Mr. Vernon spoke made me feel strong and smart. I liked hearing him talk about Lance, who'd been only a few years older than me. Lance was always a hard worker, Mr. Vernon said—built a stable for his first horse when he was only fifteen. The old man seemed to believe even a kid like me could be as great as Lance.

Sometimes he talked about his wife, too. When Lance was little, she grabbed up an axe and chased away a mad dog that was coming after him in the yard. She was proud of Mr. Vernon for being elected to the church vestry—to bring back the good family name, he said, chuckling. His father had nearly wrecked it by being a local hell-raiser, running a still, chasing after the hired girls. When I talked to him about the few things I'd heard about my own father, like how he beat up my mother and drove her crazier than she already was, Mr. Vernon gazed at me and nodded, like he understood.

After I'd been working at the farm about eight months, I finally told him about the woman I hit driving stoned in the last car I stole. She was only about 30 but after the accident she walked bent over and had to use two canes to limp to the witness stand in court. When she told the judge she couldn't keep a job now because of her constant pain, she broke down in tears, and I started shuddering, myself. Later, though, I tried to convince myself that the judge had it in for me, sending me upstate instead of extending my probation like courts always did before when I'd got busted. I ran my mouth, acting like a hot shit about my car-boosting career when I first got to camp. But that's not how I talked to Mr. Vernon. I thought that when he heard about the woman I'd run down, he'd stand up and tell me in disgust to go back to my bunk. But he stayed in the armchair facing me, letting me talk and talk.

When I'd finally dried my eyes, he looked at me sorrowfully. "I know you got to live with that story."

I nodded. "How can I?"

"Give it time, son," he said. "Give it time…."

Today I picture him in the farmhouse, easing himself up from the rocking chair by the fireplace to get a good look at me as I walk in. His gray stubble will be grown out and now he'll have a long beard that makes him look like an all-forgiving God in old Bible story books. He'll wrap his bony arms around me. "Welcome home, Pete! I knew I could depend on you to come back—just like I always could, the way you worked!

It's true, I always worked my heart out for him. He and Laurie sometimes had to tell me to go easy, stop killing myself with whatever job it was I was getting done. Laurie would tempt me inside with her strawberry-rhubarb pie, and right now I'm guessing she'll set down a piece in front of me at the kitchen table with a tall glass of lemonade. Hard to say who'll be happiest, them watching me eat or me eating.

Then the big show—I'll bring out my certificates. Who'd have thought I'd have any, a school fuck-up like me? Mr. Vernon used to worry that he was keeping me away from the camp's classes when he took me to work on the farm, but the state's "educational" program was just a way to keep us busy, using 1950s kiddy textbooks marked *REJECTED* by some school district downstate. Made sense, we were rejects, right? Everyone but me was reading at elementary level, but nobody liked being reminded of their dumbness with that Dick 'n' Jane shit. So we turned off our minds in the classrooms and took every chance we had to skip school.

I'll unroll the documents one by one on the dining room table. "See, this one's for passing all my high school courses, I'll say—*General Education High School Equivalenc" Diploma, State of New York.* The old man will crack that grin of his. "Good for you, boy!" He'll say. "I always said you were smart as a whip, didn't I say that, girls?" And Laurie and Dolores will both nod their heads like they'd always known I was smart, too.

I'll show another paper—*Diploma in Carpentry and Building Trades,* my favorite. "It's accepted by all the unions, a ticket to high-paid house-maintenance and construction jobs, there's always something needs building and fixing," I'll tell Mr. Vernon. "You were the first to teach me everything!" He'll hold onto my shoulder, smiling.

I wonder if I should show them the certificate for *Certified Drug Counselor.* I earned it on the early-release program that Frederic, my smooth-talking lawyer and his political pals fixed for me. How do you keep a Vietnam vet junkie ex-con too busy to use? You teach him how to keep other Vietnam vet junkie ex-cons from using. I worked at that counseling job for two years til it blew up in my face and I lost Raquel. But even if my hands are shaking, I'll show them the certificate, I'll tell them how hard I worked at the Crisis Center, counseling, taking case histories, running group meetings.

Now I get to a really big certificate. This one's in a gilt-flecked wood frame with glass that'll flash bright in the window light. *"State of New York, Platt County Community College Extension Program,"* I'll read it aloud, though the fancy script is big enough for anyone to see. *"Hereby grants Peter James Zachary an Associate's Degree in English and Language Arts."* And there's the big gold seal at the bottom shaped like a sun-burst. Old man Vernon will touch the glass with his fingertips, and his face will have a prouder look on it than I've ever seen before. He'll be speechless.

Laurie will pound me on the back. "You going to be an English teacher, Slick?"

"Maybe," I'll say. Though I never could be, not with my record. I won't tell her that only two degree courses were offered in that prison, Criminal Law and English, and the law program I wanted was already filled up by the time I got my GED transcript transferred. I haven't got a clue what I'll do with an Associate's Degree in English, which I already spoke fine before I signed up. Well, I can keep a journal, like I've been doing for years. I can throw around big words if I want to, though mostly I keep them to myself, why draw attention, piss people off? I did like all the novels, still do. I never messed with them in public school, I was too busy being a badass. But during my last bid I read over 200 books! They kept loneliness and craziness at bay. If those twin buzzards try to swoop down on me again, I have a box of more books in the Caddie's trunk to fend them off with.

Dolores will say, "I better be careful the way I speak English, Pedro—you might hear my bad grammar." I'll tell her there's nothing wrong with her English and there never was. Then Mr. Vernon will take a nap, knocked out by all the excitement. Dolores and Laurie and me, we'll sit out on the side porch in rocking chairs. I'll have my boots resting up on the rail, a glass of lemonade in my hand. Laurie will be barefoot, her chubby toes wriggling on the rail next to my boots. And Dolores will have on the gold sandals she liked to put on after working, her toenails painted purple. Her eyes will be half closed with her shiny black hair falling over her shoulders.

I'll ask Laurie and Dolores if they'll bring out their guitars. They'll get one for me, too, so I can strum the chords they taught me all those years ago. I'll start harmonizing once I get my voice back. It's been scratchy as hell this past month, I could hardly talk at all. For now, it'll be better to just listen to them softly humming.

The road uphill is a lot longer than I remembered it. Just around the bend…at the end of the next long field where all the parallel furrows end…. *There's the farm!* At a distance it looks the way I've seen it in my mind since I was 15—the house a white ocean liner floating on a sea of shimmering grass. The deck—the long side porch—waits for me to step onto it and sail away….

But first, I come to the barn across the road. It's weather-blasted red, and it leans more than it used to. The wide-open doorway slants like a screaming mouth. Inside is where Mr. Vernon and Laurie kept their old cars, "organ donors" Laurie used to call them, because their parts were ripped out to use in other farm vehicles. When I bragged about my daring life of crime, she said, "Slick, don't even think about swiping one of those junkers from the barn, they'd fall apart before you even got to the bottom of the hill." I never would have boosted anything from her place, of course, though I could have lots of times.

I pull off the road, staring through the barn door. No vehicles in there, no hay bales in the lofts. Some of the beams hang down at crazy angles, who knows what's holding them up. Not much of the roof left, big scraps of blue sky visible through jagged holes. I smell old straw, an itchy scent I loved even though it made my eyes sting. It still does, I still love it.

I switch off the Caddie's engine. A thousand birds twitter. They fly in and out the barn door, swoop down from the rafters, make a fluttery panic in the air I can feel against my face. The twitters swell into a mass screech. Hey, *come on, guys!* All I did was stop here—and suddenly I'm a goddamn intruder?

Gradually the noise fades, the birds get warily used to me. That's better.

I pull the Caddie as deep as I can into the barn, then struggle to close the big door to keep it out of sight. I used to slide the barn door shut on its metal track, but now, when I tug at it, the heavy panel squeaks to a halt, only closes about half way. No wonder, the track's rusted. I spot a tarp. It gives off a rubbery odor in the heat, all crumpled in a corner. When I try to pick it up to cover the Caddie, the canvas feels like dead elephant skin. I drop it fast. The car's safe enough in these shadows from being spotted. Who's going to be looking way out here in the sticks? Maybe a car a week passes by, I remember. I haven't seen one since I got here.

I step out into the daylight. Blink hard. Take a deep breath. Slowly I turn toward the house.

5

The ocean liner I saw before has shrunk to an old two-story houseboat stranded on a shaggy meadow. The clapboard siding's been scraped raw by wind and rain. Several shutters droop at angles, a few have fallen off completely. Waist-high grass grows in a ragged fringe around the building. On the second floor, squares of sunlit glass glare red like they're reflecting coals from a fire that could have swept through the rooms. I hear a long groan. My own voice.

The front walk's hardly visible beneath the grass. The old man and I collected stones from tumbled-down old walls, split them with a sledge hammer into thin layers of shale, I remember how we laid them down in a line from the road to the front step—

I have to lean over fast—dizzy spell, a *whirrrrrrrr!* in my ears which I get sometimes since Vietnam. Hunker down, press fingertips into the dirt. Rest, and it passes. I stand up, arms out at my sides for balance. I take a step toward the house—another step…raise my head.

Pillars like spindly drunks hold up the side porch's tilting roof. The railing's broken here, sagging there,

39

collapsed at the end. The porch floor's covered with layers of leaves. I breathe harder, mind racing—the girls must be too busy with their music to keep things up, maybe Mr. Vernon isn't as handy as he used to be, maybe his eyesight's going....

I rap loud on the door. No movement inside. Maybe Laurie's practicing her guitar upstairs. She and Dolores were a two-girl act, probably still are, they sang country-folk songs in the local gin mills—that's what bars are called up here—on weekends. I don't hear any music, though. Keep pounding, pounding. Paint-chips flake off the wood. I remember Mr. Vernon used to say—"Always keep your house looking shabby on the outside so when the assessors come around every year, they won't tax your property so high."

I twist the door knob and ram my shoulder against the door. And go flying inside, damn near sprawl onto the floor. The door wasn't locked! I should've remembered— Mr. Vernon and Laurie never locked the house. They used to brag about the county being so safe you never had to. At least til the raiders from the camp came. After that night, I bet everybody in the county double-locked their doors, night and day.

Blind with left-over sun-glare, I call out, *"Hey! Hello in here! It's me! I'm back!"* My voice ricochets off walls— bursts of relief that I've finally come home. I don't have to hold back anything any longer, I don't need to worry about being cagey or cautious—I can just yell my damn head off! *"Hey! Hello! Hello! Hell-ohhh!"*

My eye finally focus. Oh shit, oh shitshitshit!.... The parlor's a wreck. Faded wallpaper curls off the walls in long strips. The floor's speckled with dirty plaster fallen from the ceiling, bald spots show bare boards overhead. The air's musty, unbreathed….

No one lives here now. No one has lived here for a long time. My eyes sting with dust, tears stream down my face—

— *Aw, Slick, don't take it so hard! It's <u>been</u> a long time!*
— *You'll see us again, Pedro….*

I gulp back tears, nod at the voices in my ears, but my legs go rubbery as I cross the parlor floor. So many windows cracked, whole panes shattered! The goddamn rain's blown in, soggied an armchair, turned it lumpy. Big pieces of glass crack underfoot, a crunching sensation like walking on thin ice. I want to turn around and flee. But I can't. Where the fuck can I go? I can't go back—can't go forward! I was counting on the family to help me figure out what to do about the awful fix I'm in—to give me the strength to go on to Montreal alone—I was counting on them—

"*Hey-y-y!*" I scream, my voice ragged. I'm worn out, whacked, muscle-dead. An old habit kicks in—I plunk myself down in the armchair where I used to collapse after farm chores. But my ass drops through what's left of the cushion, my knees in the air. I'm wedged into the damn frame. "*Let go! Let me up!*" Holy shit!—that's me screaming at a chair!—

— *Hey, rock the chair! Rock sideways!*
— *Wriggle your legs! Don' give up!*
— *Do it, Slick! Keep trying!*
— *Don' give up now, Pedro!*

I picture Laurie doubling over with her arm around Dolores's shoulder, the two of them smiling down at me. I take their advice and rock. Clunk!—the chair topples sideways and spits me out. I'm free, and scramble to my feet again, heart galloping. The house is still, even the air outside's gone quiet. All those birds must have fled the barn, leaving me alone here. Just me, not a sound....

I used to love the silence. So different from the camp. All day the barracks exploded with racket—kids' threats and taunts and screams echoing in the tight cinderblock corridors. The noise battered away at my nerves, panic-alert adrenaline spraying through my brain like acid-spurts.

But here on the farm it used to get so quiet that when I stood in the road all I heard were faint chords being strummed upstairs in the house, the girls' hazy voices floating through the afternoon. Air currents carried them away...and left cool, soft *silence*....

Now the quiet in the house is different. It's not floating, it's aching through me like the constantly fading note of a gong that won't stop reverberating in my chest.

Can I really be here? How can I tell if I'm somewhere if there's nobody else to see me and listen to me and nod back at me, keeping me from feeling like nothing but a hole in the air, letting me know I've got a right to take up space in the world?

I'm feeling like a little kid staring out the window of an empty room, spooning cold spaghetti out of a can after my mother's been dragged off to the hospital again. But I never felt that way *here* before! All these years, I've held onto a memory of this beautiful house full of people who'd never let me feel like that kid again. *Where are they?*

I wrote them I was coming—I still can recite the letter! I addressed the envelope carefully in big print— RD# 1, SPRING HILL ROAD, OAK HOLLOW, NY. The same address I'd sent dozens of postcards to over the years—"Doing great. I miss you. Love to you all, Pete"—

with no return addresses, me not wanting them to know where I was at the time. But this last letter had my return address in New York City, and it didn't come back. Was it forwarded somewhere? Or did the mailman slip the envelope under the door here? Is it somewhere in the house?

The kitchen, always so white in my memory and glowing with good smells—roast beef, fried chicken, brownies—is a wreck. Shelves empty, no envelope anywhere. The refrigerator still stands against one wall, but as soon as I open it a rotted-meat stench blasts into my face. I stagger backwards, gagging. I open a window—too fast—*crack!* It smacks against the top of the frame. The whole room trembles. The glass has shattered. I grab up a piece, blood fills my palm.

Dizzy again, I sink to one knee, grab my face in both hands. The blood's sticky on my cheek. I grope for the tap in the sink, twist the knobs. Water gurgles in the pipes, flows out rusty brown. Why has water been left on here? Never mind, I hold my palm under the stream, splash my face, taste bitter rust on my lips. The water swirls pinkish brown in the drain.

I climb the stairs—same old creaks but louder. The air in the hall smells dusty, I start coughing till my eyes tear over again. Laurie and Dolores slept up here. They had separate rooms, even if they were lezzies. I never cared what they were. I even figured that since they were a couple, then there'd never be boyfriends around for me to get jealous of. Each room's bare now—no traces of the girls anywhere, not even a piece of ribbon in a corner or a bobby pin on the window sill. No letter…no letter…no letter! What the hell happened to it?

Once I helped the girls carry their instruments upstairs and got a glimpse into the rooms, the big double beds, the bright quilts thrown over them. And the posters on the wall. Laurie loved Janice Joplin, she played her records for me. When Laurie sang, her voice could sob and wail, she'd squeeze feelings out her throat that were too scary to let go full-blast. Dolores had a poster of Joan Baez over her bed. Dolores's voice was softer, with long ripples at the end of notes. A ghost of the poster's in her room—a less-sun-faded rectangular space in the faint flowery wallpaper. I rest my palm against the space for a while, fingers stroking where the dark hair was.

Under one broken window is a bird's nest, no eggs or shells, just a little cup of straw, empty, empty. That can't be all that's left in the house, can it? I rush back downstairs, stop in front of the door to the room where Laurie and the old man did their bill-paying and farm work-planning, and Laurie made her calls to line up music gigs. They called the room the office. Occasionally Mr. Vernon slept on a daybed in there when he felt too tired to drive back over the hill to the house he used to share with his wife and his son.

Against one wall stood a roll-top desk with lots of little honey-comb slots where the old man kept important papers. My letter could be there. The farm's cash was kept in the upper left-hand drawer. I knew this because once when I was sweeping the office I saw a stack of bills a couple inches thick in that open drawer. I made a lot of noise cleaning up in there because I wanted Laurie and Mr. Vernon to know I was near the money but wasn't touching it.

A long rifle rested on two pegs on the wall. A thirty-ought-six, Mr. Vernon called it. Laurie used to tease him about the gun, saying it was an antique like he was, nobody could ever hit anything with it. "Well, we'll just see about that," he whispered to me. Then we tromped together out into a field where woodchucks had been digging holes, which Mr. Vernon said were dangerous for livestock that could step into and break a leg. He shot two "chucks" with that old rifle. He even showed me how to sight along the barrel and squeeze the trigger—*me,* a convicted felon! Anyway, when the gun exploded, I thought the stock had smashed my shoulder bones, but after some more shots, I learned how to cradle it right and absorb the kick. I didn't hit any animals, but I knew I'd never forget the feel of that rifle's heft in my hands.

Laurie had a big grin on her face when we got back with the woodchucks. "Way to go, Dad!" she said, whacking him on the shoulder. His lined cheeks rippled when he smiled. Laurie told me later that the gun was the first thing he'd shown any real enthusiasm for after his wife's and Lance's deaths. She said she was real glad I'd taken him out shooting, it was just what he needed.

When we went back inside the office, he rested the gun back up on the pegs where I could see it. He trusted me. They all did.

Look, something about that office door seems different from the rest of the house….

There, on the floor—a fan-shaped scrape in the wood. Plaster dust has been pushed away by the movement of the door's bottom edge. That door's been opened recently! Someone's been here—and not too long ago! I picture a person—Mr. Vernon? Laurie? Dolores?—reaching out, taking hold of the round china doorknob, twisting it, pulling it open. The door would make a little screech as its bottom skids along the floor. I can almost hear its echo.

Is the daybed still in there? The desk?

Is the rifle resting on the wall pegs?

I stare hard at the door, take a step toward it.

6

The doorknob's strangely warm, like the hand of someone who's eager to shake mine. I pull it, and the door greets me with a sigh—yes, the bottom edge dragging across the floorboards. The room's pretty much like I pictured it—bed and desk, black phone on the desk, and two pegs that poke out of the wall, square eyes, blank stares. But no rifle's mounted there.

The ceiling's plaster is scabbed and peeling…but why are there so many fewer flakes on the floor in this room than the others? Has someone been sweeping in here? A stick-figure broom watches me from a corner. It's pretty new, the straws still yellow, the handle shiny blue.

Somebody's sure as hell been here. A week ago? A month? A year? And who? Search for clues. The desk's cubby holes are empty. No letter, shit, I guess I can forget about finding it anywhere. The top drawer where I'd once seen the money won't open. I poke the dusty lock, knowing I could pop it easy, but I don't want anyone to find it and think I tried to rob the family. With the flashlight from the Caddie, I shine a beam under the desk. Cobweb jungle. But something glitters. I pull it out and cup it in the blood-smeared palm of my hand. A tiny flat bird made of tin, painted shiny blue, its wings outspread. It's the one Dolores glued to her guitar—to help it sing, she said, a Mexican feathered spirit. Laurie and Dolores were into Indian lore—sacred creatures, dream-catchers and all that. I rub the bird gently against my shirt, feeling the pointy wings, then tuck it deep into my pants pocket.

Far under the desk I find a tiny plastic bottle whose label reads "Walter Vernon." I never knew the old man was called "Walter." Laurie—and Dolores, too—always called him "Dad." I wanted to, too, but never quite dared. I blow the dust off the label. "July 1, 1971," it says. That was when I was at the camp—just a few weeks before I left! Almost exactly eleven years ago. "To be taken immediately at onset of heart palpitations." There's still several pills clicking around inside the bottle. I had no idea he had heart trouble. He did shuffle around the barracks at night but he moved faster when Laurie was around, like he didn't want her to see him dragging his feet. He wasn't all that old, though he looked craggy—maybe 55 or 60, since Laurie was 25. The way he moved wasn't because of age, it was because a tractor tipped over on him once and crushed his leg, he told me. He'd dragged himself half a mile to his house to phone for help.

I move to the daybed, and—how could I have missed it, hiding in plain sight?—there's Laurie's *serape!* Red, green, black, yellow stripes. They're faded, but it's the same Mexican shawl Dolores gave Laurie for her birthday. I remember Laurie lifting it out of the box. The sunlight soaked into it, making the colors glow like a church window. Laurie gave Dolores a big hug to thank her. She wore it everywhere. When I carried the girls' guitars and amps out to the pickup truck for their music gigs—a roadie, they called me—she always had it on. Now I can stroke the *serape* like I used to dream of doing. It's as soft as it looked, even after all this time.

— *Hey, Slick, you're blushing!*

— *Is okay, Pedro, you don' got to be shamed of nothing!*

I spread it over the mattress again and fall onto it like dropping out of a cloud.

When I wake, it's dark. I've been losing track of day and night recently. Sitting on the front step with the *serape* folded in my lap, I stare into the deep black air. I can't even see the tree next to the house, only hear the branches blowing *scratch-scratch, scratch-scratch,* long claws scraping wood siding. Through the open window, the sky's a black tent stretched high above the barn roof, pin-pricks of light flicker through the tarp. Smells are stronger at night. The green scent of the long grass. Wildflowers somewhere. I push my nose into the *serape* and recall again that warm flannel-shirt-and-sweat scent of Laurie, me, and Dolores riding squashed together on the pickup's front seat. Then I raise my head and I'm sure I can smell tacos and enchiladas cooking in the kitchen. I'm hungry, starving.

I get my cheap food out of the Caddie. The money I put into restoring this car! My counseling salary, all the under-the-counter construction jobs I took nights and weekends. I kept my money stash, plus Raquel's smaller one, locked in the trunk, it was going to cover our first months in Montreal. I never planned to have that cellophane-wrapped brick of cash squashed under the spare tire, but now I'm aware of it like a heavy stone in my gut. Who knows how much money's there? A Franklin's on top, maybe there's all 100s underneath, too. I haven't even unwrapped it and don't want to if I can help it. I know what it could buy. Albany's not that far away, show me any city, I can find my way to a dealer in no time. It's been two years, but I still feel rushes of longing, twitches and screams in my veins—especially this last horrible month.

I bring my blankets inside. I can stay just one night, what's the harm? I wolf down some cheese sandwiches and head to the office. I don't want to get Laurie's *serape* dirty, sleeping on it, so I tuck it under the desk's roll top. Then I lay out my blankets on the scratchy mattress. But I can't sleep. I should have grabbed a book from the Caddie. *Crime and Punishment*, my favorite bedtime story. Outdoors, the peepers cry their tiny hearts out for their froggy mamas, and the crickets are having orgies in the grass. I don't mind the critter sounds keeping me company, especially with no other houses for several miles in all directions. I like being isolated here. But it can get damn spooky, too!

When I wake up again, the daylight's roasting the air, making me sweat. Outside the window, something screeches like a piece of metal shoved into a table saw blade. It's just a kind of bug…a cicada. Once Mr. Vernon showed me the dried skin of one at the base of a tree trunk. It looked like a transparent plastic shell, an exact 3-D copy of the insect, head and bulbous tail, legs with crooked elbows that seem about to make the thing spring into the air and fly away.

"How could it have wriggled out of its skin?" I once asked the old man. "I wish I could do that."

He nodded. "I know…."

I shuffle around fighting off gloom, exploring. Upstairs I find an empty lipstick tube in a closet corner. Another souvenir. Laurie never used make-up so this must be Dolores's. She liked to make her pouty lips purple, to bring out the color of her skin, she said.

When I first saw Raquel walk into the group therapy session that I ran, my jaw dropped—she had the same golden complexion and dark full mouth as Dolores. She even had the Latina accent. From the start I loved listening to her voice in that group, a flute in a circle of groaning tubas. Weeks later, when I heard her making those high notes close up, her lips brushing my ear on the pillow, I felt tiny pings go off inside me, miniature firecrackers in my muscles. Raquel's and my apartment in New York was no bigger than a trailer. It had one window that looked out on a courtyard where colored shirts and pants swayed in the air, goofy clowns dancing from clotheslines. We raised the window to feel the breeze. Raquel's damp hair stuck to her cheeks. She liked to practice her English as I pointed to things outside. *"Pants, shirt, towel, cloud, bird."* The courtyard seemed alive with normal, amazing objects, each one having its own sound that made halting, pretty music in her mouth. Her lips shaped them carefully as if tasting each one. *Ween-dow, cloze-lyon.* When I told her, "Yes, good, that's right," she smiled up into my face. My finger slid down her *wreest* to her *nook-els!* What? "Don' laugh!" she cried out, but she was laughing, too—*"nook-els!"*—and she pummeled the air above her head like a boxer, her breasts quivering. Her eyes crinkled like this was too much happiness for her to bear.

But sometimes, in the circle of chairs in the Group Room at the Center, I heard sour, tearful words from her, about when she first came from the Dominican Republic to live with her uncle. His sons were always after her, she couldn't get away. They raped her when she was fourteen, fifteen, until she slashed one of them across the groin with a straight razor, aiming for his dick. She couldn't tell her uncle about the boys, she said, because he worked so hard to keep her in a good Catholic high school, then City College. He was kind to her, she said, but he didn't sound too terrific to me. He thought his sons were great kids, and never caught on that they were tormenting Raquel or dealing heroin out of his house. Or that they were starting her on it.

"When I got high, they didn't hurt so much," she said.

I had to listen and let her rage and terror tumble out, I couldn't stroke her hair away from her eyes or blot the tears streaming down her face. I had to be the counselor, using a new language, counselor-ese. Sometimes it was all I had to keep her from bolting the group. I tried not to speak that way in our apartment when her black mood-clouds came down, drenching her in despair.

But she still cut her eyes at me. "You talk like you got it all together, like you think you better'n me!" she said.

I said, "Of course I don't! You're just having bad spell, that's all."

She tilted her head and said, "Thas bullshit, Petey."

I knew it was, too, but I couldn't face what she really needed—some miraculous way to stop drowning in her own gloom.

"Maybe now and then, we jus skin-pop, you know?" she asked me. "Nothin in the veins, just somethin to take away these goddamn blahs?"

I kept telling her, "No no no no no—*we can't go there!*"

She stopped turning up at meetings. I got on her case, asked her where she'd been, what she'd been doing.

"You don' control what I do, Petey!" she screamed. "Leave me the fuck *alone* sometimes! Jus' for a while— *okay?*"

And I did leave that day, I left her screaming at me. I wandered the streets, trying to plan how to get her back into the program, back to me.

I pace the house, squeeze the lipstick tube so tight the edge digs a circle into my palm. It stings, feels sharp like something alive, it clears my head. I think about Dolores like I used to--laughing, trying out a new song, her voice quavering as she strummed chords. Once, after she'd blotted her lips and tossed the tissue onto the kitchen counter, I secretly slipped it into my pocket. Back in the barracks at camp, I unfolded it and saw the purple lip-print on the soft paper. It smelled sweet like lipstick, too. I was ashamed of what I did with it under my blanket.

But if she'd known, she would've probably just laughed.

— *Pedro, stop worry, you always give yourself such a rough time!*

I laugh, too, now. My loud voice startles the hell out of me in the empty house. I put the little lipstick tube on an old crate beside the office bed. Then I sweep the upstairs, then the porch, and take away arm-loads of dead leaves. My back aches, but it's a good feeling, like the way I used to feel after haying or mucking out the barn for Mr. Vernon.

In the bathroom mirror, I glimpse myself all coated with dirt from the leaves. The shower stall's a trough of plaster scabs, and when I turn the knobs, brown water dribbles out. What if Dolores and Laurie and Mr. Vernon come back and find me like this? I'll never get clean enough here. But I don't want to drive back to the truck stop, it's too risky after the way I fucked everything up at that woman's store.

There was a pond in one of the fields where I used to wash off after work. Staring out the window, I spot what looks like a shiny patch of silver foil in the tall grass. It must be that pond, but why's it so small? Probably because in eleven years it got overgrown by weeds and algae. They clog up the water if nobody takes care of it, Mr. Vernon always said as I glopped out the green muck on the prongs of his rake.

I wade barefoot through the field, the tall grass swishing against my legs, and approach the pond not in a straight line but along a winding, invisible path. There *was* a path out here, I remember now, and my feet still know to follow it. I come to Lance's Dock. That's what Mr. Vernon called the dock him and his son built. Once me and the old man stood on those boards staring at the water and he said, "When I come out here alone, I look down and see the reflections of both of us." That gave me the shivers because sure enough, two figures were rippling there on the surface of the pond, but the younger one wasn't Lance. Or was he?

The boards of the dock sag, slanted right down to the pond's surface. Water sparkles in the sunlight. I pull off my clothes, ease myself in. It's warm as a bath. When I move my feet, tiny bubbles swarm up like minnows nibbling at my skin. I wade around rubbing my face and hair and body, trying to get clean. Funny how I used to be scared of the plants on the bottom, they felt like snakes wriggling under my toes. And the first time I saw some frogs, I jumped back and asked Laurie, Hey, do those things bite? You could have heard that brassy laugh of hers all down the valley.

Dolores whispered to me that she used to be scared of frogs, too.

Then Laurie ruffled my hair. "We'll make a slouter out of you yet," she said. A "slouter" was a hillbilly who kept rusted cars in the yard around his cabin, tied up a mean dog on his front stoop, shot deer out of season. It was what country people called each other in a jokey way, sort of like "redneck," but outsiders better not say it near them or they'd get fighting mad. So when Laurie told me I'd be a slouter, I felt happy that she was going to include me among the people who belonged here.

The girls kept inner-tubes on the pond's bank to float around on, big bulgy rubber doughnuts whose hole you could sink deep into with your ass cooling in the water. Late one afternoon, I walked out there in just my jeans, drag-footed with tiredness from work, and flopped down backwards onto a tube. I heard a little splash at the other side of the pond. There was Laurie, floating in a tube, too, gazing at the sky. I smelled something sweet. She was smoking a joint.

I wasn't sure she even knew I was there. She had nothing on but a thin undershirt and polka-dotted underpants. Her knees stuck up, her arms drooped beside her into the water. I kept glancing at her tits in the nearly transparent wet cotton—no more grapefruits now but two plump white fish resting on her chest, noses big and dark and curious. Now her tube floated closer to mine. Her eyes opened, a sleepy smile drifted across the water. I wonder if she saw my hard-on in my wet jeans. All she did was pluck the joint from her lips and flop her arm out toward me. So I took the joint and sucked in a long toke.

We lay suspended there in the water, tubes bumping softly as we passed the dope back and forth without a word. The sun never felt so warm, the water so silky. Staring at the sky, I felt like Laurie and I were up there gliding along with the clouds. I dozed off, faded into the blue. When I woke up, Laurie was gone, but in a way she's been floating beside me ever since.

I spend another night on the bed, waking up over and over. The baby frogs and the crickets have gone to sleep, and the quiet's back. Once I walk outdoors and stand in the middle of the road with the house on one side and the barn on the other under the speckled sky. It's so dark I can't see where the road came from or where it leads to. I can hardly remember how I got to this once-upon-a-time world, this "Garden of Eden" as Dolores called it. After a while a silver toenail of a moon pokes out of the sky just above the barn's roof--God's toenail. The rest of him is standing above the giant black circus tent, a bearded ogre as tall as the solar system. Is he frowning down at me through the little rip his toenail's made in the black canvas? No. I'd be smaller than a gnat to him, littler than a gnat's left ball, tinier than a dust-mote on the gnat's left ball.

The next morning, I know I ought to leave. But I put it off. I sit on the front step and write in my journal, page after page fills up with Raquel again, keeping her alive on paper and draining away enough pain to let me go on for a while, that's what the journal's been for, this past month. I take my weights out of the Caddie and do my 85-minute workout on the porch til I can feel my legs and arms and chest get warm, but somehow they don't lose their jumpiness. I pace around the house until I start to feel sick and dizzy from the moldy smells and plaster dust.

Finally I take out the *serape*, spread it carefully over the day bed's scratchy old mattress. At least the room's got a more cheerful look now, the *serape* colors tinting the air.

But the rest of the house—I can't stand it any longer. I can't squint into the light streaming in the parlor windows onto the wreckage—like a bombed out building, walls and ceiling ripped to shreds, the floorboards stripped and filthy. The air's compressed, echoing so loud I want to clap my hands over my ears. This isn't the first bombed-out building I've wandered through, rubbing my eyes, growing sicker and sicker at the stench…. Does it really stink *that* bad in here—Vietnam bad?

I pack my car in five minutes, just heaving stuff into the trunk and mashing it down. As I careen down the road, the brown dust-clouds swirl in the rear view mirror. At the bottom of the hill, I think I know my way back to the highway that leads to Montreal…but I don't. After a while the Caddie turns onto a winding blacktop that I realize I've taken years before.

I'm headed toward a place called the Glen Castle Hotel, the fanciest resort in the mountains, Laurie told me. It was beautiful, it looked like that place my mother once told me about, maybe it even was the same hotel. Wings fanned out from the sprawling white main building, curved shingled roofs swooped over verandahs. Behind it, at the edge of the wide lawn, a stream splashed out of the woods into a waterfall that pushed a big wooden mill wheel round and round.

Laurie and Dolores played a gig there one summer afternoon. I was their roadie again, lugging the equipment into the big dining room where they set up. Its walls were painted with scenes of shepherd-girls in half-open dresses dancing in circles, with goat-legged guys ogling their asses from behind trees. The room was packed with people, and a long mirror behind the bar created another room mobbed with their twins. The French doors opened out onto the grass which was so green and pretty you expected a flock of shepherd-girls to come skipping over it with plump pink tits a-bobbing. Actually some of the women in the audience outdoors were sunbathing topless, along with shirtless guys with snaggly long hair, everybody passing wine bottles and joints around. This was as close as I got to the hippie-fests I used to hear about in those days. Some local folks were there, too, men in their overalls and feed-caps, wives in baggy jeans and checked shirts looking embarrassed but clapping their hands as the music pulsed out of the big room. The air was swirling with sweet reefer smoke, talk about contact high, even some of those Farmer Browns had illicit smiles on their faces.

That was when I heard Laurie and Dolores do "Me and Bobby Mcgee," a song that got rowdier as it galloped along til several guys jumped up onstage with guitars. The drummer smashed the cymbals so fast his arms turned blurry like helicopter blades. Inside and outside, everybody was singing along, someone set the dining room chandeliers swinging in sync with the people swaying in the audience. I couldn't tell if Bobby was a guy or a girl, it didn't matter. Laurie had undone her yellow braid so that her hair flowed down her shoulders and splashed around with Dolores's silky black curls as they sang, heads together, swaying. It was beautiful.

Later, the girls showed me the chords for that song, even lent me a guitar to practice on back at the camp. A lot of nights it kept me from going nuts in that place. "Bobby Mcgee" was the first song I learned. I pictured having a girlfriend to travel the lonesome roads with, sometimes she looked like Laurie, sometimes Dolores, or sometimes it was a guy, an older brother I could always count on.

One famous line was about freedom meaning nothing left to lose. It took me years to really figure that out. I think you have to wander the city streets with the freedom to burrow into any ripe dumpster you choose for dinners, to sleep under any bridge you want. Or find yourself AWOL from your unit in Vietnam with a heroin jones coming down and your girlfriend gone from the house, the clothes you bought her dumped in the commode, and the grim-eyed neighbors jabber-jabbering at you when you wander from hutch to hutch saying her name, sure they know where she is but won't ever, ever tell you.

And years later, the day after Raquel's funeral, I went back to our apartment and saw nothing left to lose there— furniture, pictures, plates, flower pots, pans. I threw stuff out the window, the metal things clanked down the fire escape. I gave away as much as I could and left the rest. But the real nothing-left-to-lose was me. I couldn't wait to be free of me.

Finally I ease into the curve toward the hotel…and there it is, sprawling, gabled, tall…but damn!—so fucking gloomy now! The dark mountainside behind it is a sky-high shadow. The clapboard siding's no longer cream white but bleached-out boards. The yard's overgrown with spiny weeds. The French doors are all curtained, the long row of windows upstairs shuttered. What the hell *is* it about this country and the buildings here? What's happened? It feels like all the places shut down on purpose when they somehow heard I was coming. My teeth grind hard. I pick up speed along the curve, leave the place behind.

I keep driving the back roads all afternoon, taking a final look around the countryside. The car rolls along finding its own way, and after a while it's taking me past the Oak Hill cemetery. I brake just beside the angels and get out. They look welcoming with their wings spread, the slanting rays of sunlight turning stone into soft ivory-tinted skin. But the way they gaze at me out of those blank eyes makes me sad.

"*Adios*, ladies," I say. "I'll miss you."

Why are you leaving? the nearest angel asks, her voice whispery.

"Might be somebody's after me. Staying's too risky."

Life is like that, the other angel whispers. *Risky. Always was.*

"There's nothing to stay for."

What is there to leave for?

"I couldn't find what I came looking for. They're gone—Mr. Vernon, Laurie, Dolores."

How do you know?

You could wait for them to come back to the house.

You could go looking for them.

You haven't tried that.

"It's no good. Their house's a wreck. Nobody's taken care of it for years."

You could clean it, fix it up nice.

It's the least you could do for them.

"Listen, it's empty—*abandoned!*"

He's chickening out, the nearest angel whispers to the other. *Listen to him!* Is that laughter I hear in her voice?

He's giving up already, the other one whispers, also sounding chirpy. *Giving up….*

"Hey, ladies—I don't need you getting on my case—"

Yes, you do!

You didn't give up on Raquel.

Did I tell them about Raquel? I don't remember, I must have. "Yeah, and look what happened to her!"

Are you sorry you kept trying?

Do you wish you'd given up on her?

"Hell, no!" I step back, wiping my eyes. "That's got nothing to do with…staying here!"

Bullshit!

Bullshit!

I didn't know angels used that kind of language. I squint from face to stone face. "What'd you mean?"

You know.

You know.

Silence. Leaves rustle in the trees just beyond the wrought-iron fence.

The sky slowly reddens, tinting the graves. I stare at the obelisk for a long time, like it's a sundial, its pointy shadow inching along the grass. When I look up, the angels are still watching me, watching, waiting.

"Maybe I'll…spend another night. Just sleep on it," I say. "How's that?"

Silence. Shadows flicker across their faces. Are those smiles in the worn stone?

By the time I finally drive up to the house, it's so dark I can barely find my way to the office where the daybed is. My shin strikes the bed's frame. I roll onto my side, the mattress gives beneath me, scratchy. I start to doze, then open my eyes fast.

Getting to my feet, I hold the mattress for balance. Why does it feel so scratchy?

I find the flashlight on the desk, sweep a beam of light along the wall, over the rifle pegs. The beam drops onto the mattress.

What happened to the beautiful colored stripes? They're gone! The *serape*'s gone!

7

I jump to my feet, go stumbling all over the house—*"Mr. Vernon! Laurie! Dolores!"* The names echo in the rooms. I listen for sounds upstairs, downstairs, outdoors. Footprints on the dusty floorboards are indecipherable, maybe just mine. I sniff the air for people smells. Am I losing what's left of my mind?

I roam around outdoors in the dark, into fields and woods until—how many hours have passed?—the dawn light glows through a drifting mist.

Colors seep into the landscape, the grass glows a liquid green, makes me squint. The air's squabbly with the twitters of birds. Why do they always sound so alarmed when I'm around?

I jump in the Caddie, skid out of the barn in reverse. If the girls are still in this area, they might be staying with Mr. Vernon in his house about four miles away. The road takes a familiar dip where the house should be, tall weathered shingle…but what's there is a vinyl-sided ranch house, a stranger's name on the mailbox. *Shit!* I spin around, tires screeching.

Into my side view mirror glides a familiar-looking car. Was it the one I spotted outside the old woman's store? It drops back now…black, bulbous, an old Ford Crown Victoria, the kind troopers used before they switched to Chevys. It's got no bar-flashers on top, though it could be an unmarked patrol vehicle. I once read somewhere, You can never be too paranoid. Got that right.

I swerve off the road behind some bushes and roll to a stop. If that car's tailing me, it'll pass. No Crown Vic rolls by. I'm beginning to doubt I ever even saw the damn car.

Objects seen in mirror are less real than they appear.

Arriving at Laurie's house, I see the pond flickering in the sunlight, but dully, like it's about to blink out of sight. I'm not about to let that pond be overgrown. I grab an old rake I found under the porch and start mucking it out. My wet clothes get slimy with algae so I pull them all off, the water feels cooler against my bare skin. I dive and dive, scraping up handfuls of soggy gunk from the depths. I leap up to the surface, laughing, waving the dripping green stalks high in the air like slain sea monsters. The job takes all day, but I hardly notice. Clearing out this great watery pit feels like the best thing I've done in weeks.

The next morning, I buy cleaning supplies in a store far down the road in a town too big for anyone to wonder what an outsider's doing there. I scrub the house floors and even the walls with my new mop and wash the windows that aren't broken. Now the sunbeams shine in brighter. After a while the moon's watching over me. I finish the office windows by the light of a new kerosene lamp. The oil's a clear luminous blue in the lamp's glass base, the flame gives off a flowery scent.

It reminds me all in a rush of Raquel's shampoo as I washed her hair in the tub. Moonlight glowed behind the blue plastic curtains. The suds foamed down her back. I rubbed my cheek against her shoulders, so slippery, warm. Now I sit on the day bed, my face in my hands, and picture her glowing blue in the dark behind my eyelids.

At the desk, I pick up the old phone's receiver, and listen hard. A long tunnel of silence. God, I'd love to hear Raquel's voice at the other end, tell her about mucking out the pond. I'd like to phone Laurie, describe my Caddie, have her put Dolores on the line, tell her about the tin bird. Sure, and I could talk to my mother in some great celestial clinic. And while I'm at it, why not phone my father, wherever in Hell he might be?

How about I call my old lawyer—Hey Frederick, get me off again, will you? But off *what?* Am I a wanted man? Am I legal or illegal, or do I have to wait all my life in this limbo in between to find out?

I remember Frederick and the detectives in the courthouse corridor, wheeling and dealing. With his half-bored nasal voice, my attorney lorded it over the loud guys in their shiny gumshoes. He was on loan from a fancy law firm working *pro bono* among the perps and cops. I could see he liked being around loud guys, it was his thrill of the week. Still, he was clever, he saw how this work could help him with the politicians who cut deals with his firm. What a great deal for me, he said, getting released to take the training course for the drug counseling job. I could see that political connections weren't all he wanted. He wanted to *rescue* me. To give me a chance at…*redemption!* He knew my weak spot and he went for it with a harpoon.

I squeeze the phone receiver against my ear, sure I hear something at the far end of the tunnel. Somebody clearing his throat, giving me time to speak. Mr. Vernon did that.

"I took the early release deal," I tell him, closing my eyes. "I thought I could help people. Then Raquel came into the clinic and I believed I could save her, change her life—"

I hunch over the desk and tell Mr. Vernon about Raquel, and then about the afternoon when I came home to find her sprawled on the bed. One bare arm lay flopped over the edge of the mattress. Her hair splashed black on the pillow, her pupils were rolled far back in their sockets. A needle hung from the crook of her bare arm, a shiny, sucking insect gorged with dark blood. She was gone.

I ran crazy all over the streets, stumbled in and out of a bodega, raced across a little park. Spotted the junkies who hung out at the far corner, heads bobbing behind the hedge. *Who sold the shit to Raquel? Who did it? Who?* They tried to scramble away, but I grabbed a guy and knocked him to the ground. *Who? Tell me, you scumbag motherfucker! Who?* I crunched my fist into his face. One of his bitches tried to yank me off of him. *It was that cop!* She screamed at me—*that lootenant! The one at your clinic place! The place Raquel goes!* They kept crying his name—*Rand! It was Rand!* My program director—*he* was the one who'd been slinging smack he confiscated from street dealers! And selling it to Raquel!

I lurched along the street again, around the corner, into the ugly brick building where I'd run the counseling sessions. Rand's office was locked. I grabbed up a chair and smashed it through the frosted window in the door. The office was empty! My hands itched to grab him by the throat, shatter his head against the floor, strangle the breath out of him. I staggered down the steps to the basement locker room where I knew he kept stuff. From the janitor's office I grabbed a hammer and screw-driver, broke into Rand's locker in seconds. The metal door clanged backwards.

Then I saw them—the glassine packets of white powder. Five stacks of them. The shit that had killed Raquel! And beside the packets, a thick brick of cash—rubber-banded, shrink-wrapped. I snatched up a glassine bag for evidence, but where the hell would I take it—to the *police?*

"I just lost my mind, Mr. Vernon!" I sob into the phone. "I flung the bag against the wall. It exploded, a goddamn snowstorm all over the place! I ran like hell. I couldn't hardly see. I swear I didn't even know I had the brick of money in my hand til I got to my car!"

I lean back in old wooden chair turning Dolores's tin bird over and over in my palm. The lantern globe's sooty and the light's sepia-tinted, the walls barely visible around me. This little office is my home now, but sometimes it seems like a cabin in a stalled ship that just floats in place, no wind to nudge it along. Like the sailing ship in a long poem I read in an English course I took in prison. I know what that solitary sailor in the poem felt like. For shooting down a bird with an arrow, he was being punished by having to drift all alone. I think he was paying for other crimes, too, ones he couldn't even name. (For years I had a dream that just as I was packing to leave camp, a staff member kicked my suitcase away, told me my discharge papers hadn't been signed after all, the superintendent had discovered offenses of mine I hadn't known about before, so now I had to stay in camp longer, probably forever, to pay for them.) Anyway, the sailor's crimes put him under a curse that left him with a hole inside, like me—always lacking something I can't remember, I can only sense its absence.

I light the corncob pipe I bought. The smoke smells spicy, sweet, familiar. "There were times I could almost forget the curse." I say to Mr. Vernon. "Times when I was living with Raquel…and before that, those twelve months when I worked on the farm with you and Laurie and Dolores. I never felt empty then, never felt cursed."

Silence. Finally I set the receiver back in its cradle and stare at the bird in my palm. The bird in the poem was a magical creature. I've got one of my own now and it's as shiny blue as when it flashed on Dolores's guitar as she sang. I spot a tiny hole in its wing. From the Caddie's trunk I take Raquel's silk-covered jewelry box and find a thin silver chain she used to wear a gold cross on. I thread the chain through the wing's hole, then dangle the bird over one of the pegs where Mr. Vernon's rifle used to rest. Now the bird's close enough to the bed to watch over me, and near enough to the window so that, if it wants to, it can snap the tiny silver thread and fly out beneath the glass with its long blue tail flashing behind it.

The lantern's burned almost down, its wick flickering. I feel the blanket against my arm. How long have I been sleeping? I never know any more.

What happened to the *serape?* What *happened* to it?

There have to be clues about it in this room. My hunting knife's lying next to the lantern. I slip its blade under the desk-top and click open the drawer's locking mechanism. Who says you can't pick up useful skills in state correctional facilities?

The drawer's packed with old bills dated 1970 and '71, the time I was working for Mr. Vernon, and a few weeks afterwards. Then they stopped coming! *Why?* I find some newspaper clippings under the bills. They're more cheerful. Here's a black-and-white photo of Mr. Vernon as a young guy with plastered-down hair and a determined smile. He's standing with his wife, who's got a round face like Laurie's, her hair fluffy and her mouth bent in a smile. Look, here's another picture of the family standing in front of a church. Mr. Vernon's a lot older, dignified in his suit and wide tie. Mrs. Vernon's staring off with a vacant look. There's Lance, between them—high-cheeked, a buzz-cut, standing tall and crisp in an army uniform. His face is too fresh, too young for that intense serious gaze. By his side, Laurie has on a striped dress, it's the only time I've seen her in anything but jeans. She's smiling up at her brother, her eyes lit up, beautiful. *Local Family Bids Good-bye to Patriot Son* says the caption.

I turn over another clipping. Damn—a photo of the camp barracks! Dirty smudges of tear-gas leaking out the broken windows. The short newspaper article says there was a "disturbance" at the facility. Nothing about how the riot started, nothing about all the shit that went down that night til the police got there to "take command," to "quell" the trouble. I'm not really surprised that so little got reported. The state knows how to cover its ass. The newspaper wanted everybody to believe that all the camp's troubles were over with.

8

Before the riot, a lot of guys at the camp were scared shitless of Wayne. He wasn't big or strong or good at fighting. He acted crazy. Or he *was* crazy. Nobody could tell which—that was what made him so scary, and he knew it. He'd explode a soda can against a wall beside your head or slash your mattress with his shiv, then just walk away grinning. He had an off-balance swagger that made you think he was going to veer into you, then when you dodged him he'd chuckle on his way past.

Since I was his bunk-mate, on the top mattress, I had to smell him. He didn't wash much, and the greasy hair that flopped over his eyes stank like spoiled milk. At night I had to listen to him rant about tortures—pliers, razor blades, needles—he wanted to use on his father, the camp staff, other enemies. He never shut up, a fountain of diarrhea bubbling under my bunk.

But me and Wayne had an arrangement. He was the only white kid—there were about 12 of us out of 60 guys—who the blacks and Ricans never pounded on. They couldn't get back at the all-white staff who liked to do "routine restraint procedures" on them that made them pass out from being neck-locked from behind. So the blacks and Ricans scapegoated white kids. But Wayne they left alone. And they listened when he told them to lay off a kid—or to do the opposite.

The reason he had special status was that everybody wanted the pictures he drew. He could swirl his pencil-point around on a paper and all of a sudden a girl would appear wearing nothing but a bandolier of skulls crisscrossing her tits. Or she could be lying with her legs spread apart with a giant lizard tonguing her cunt, or she might be gagging on a superhero's cock. Guys would spend their week's pay for these pictures. Some of the staff tried to catch Wayne selling his artwork, but others gave him extra privileges to make drawings for them.

Pressure on him got tight, though, after the camp superintendent found a drawing of a giant pig butt-fucking his wife. So Wayne had to lie low. He said he needed a mailman and he'd make the job worth my while. One night I boosted some manila envelopes from the camp office, each one with the official NEW *YORK STATE DEPARTMENT OF YOUTH REHABILITATION SERVICES* stamp in the corner. I put Wayne's pictures in them for his customers, a nickel a delivery. The money wasn't as important as the protection. The word went out—nobody fuck with Wayne's mailman. I did my route in the evenings after working on the farm.

Wayne was curious about the place, he'd heard two hippie chicks lived there. I told him a little about Laurie and Dolores, more than I should have. When he asked me if the girls smoked dope, I said, "Hell, yeah! They grow the stuff in the garden behind their barn!"

"No shit!" He grinned. "How far from here do they live?"

I shut up. But he kept asking me, "How do you get there? How do you get there?"

"Fuck you—you *don't* get there!" I told him. "Just forget it!"

But he wouldn't. He found a local map in the camp library and figured out where the farm was. That night he lay on his back, kicking my mattress from underneath, saying, "We gotta go on a raid!" He'd jimmied open a window and knew an escape route under the camp fence. We could get to the farm in an hour, he figured, and be back around midnight.

"Stay away from that place! You'll get lost or picked up by the cops on the road!"

Wayne laughed. "If you don't come with me, I tell the niggers it's open season on your skinny white ass."

That gave me a shudder. I knew I didn't stand a chance against guys who'd been brawling on ghetto streets all their lives. They pretty much ran the camp. Even though the staff got on their case a lot, they let them get away with a lot, too. Because of The Deal. It went—You black and Rican leaders keep the peace in here for us, and we won't bother you too much about what you get up to. Later, I found out all facilities had a Deal like that between guards and inmates.

I told Wayne I wasn't going on any raid.

"Okay, you fucking pussy, I'll bring Rincon." Wayne leaned over my bunk, his smelly hair hanging down. "Keep your mouth shut. You know what happens to snitches—"

A little later, Wayne slipped out of his bunk, leaving behind a dummy made of his pajamas and a pillow under his blankets. The bastard could walk without making footsteps, I swear. I couldn't sleep. For a while I talked with Mr. Vernon, as usual.

No, not as usual at all. He told me things that shook me up, things that I'll never forget.

Then he did his rounds. Around 1:00 Wayne and Rincon snuck back in. Much later that night, I found out they'd wrapped the old man up with duct tape like a mummy and left him in his truck. In the dorm, each of them held up two pillowcases stuffed with marijuana plants.

"Get your money out, assholes!" Wayne shouted. "We're gonna get stoned tonight!"

The other midnight-to-eight staff member, Murdock, always slept through most of his shift on an empty bunk at the end of the row. That night he woke up fast. "Hey, you little shits!" he bellowed. "Stay in your bunks!"

Four kids frog-marched him down the hall. From my top bunk I could see them cramming him into a locker upside down. *Clank!*—the metal door shut on him. They must have twisted him into a human pretzel.

"Get your money out!" Wayne screamed.

Fat chance! Rincon was passing out handfuls for free. Down went Wayne as the guys ripped the pillowcases out of his hands. Joints were rolled out of any kind of paper. Contraband matches flared in the shadows. The barracks filled with smoke. Clouds of it floated everywhere. "*Aaayiiii!*" the Ricans screamed, stampeding down the hall. Black guys roamed around the bunks, laughing, slapping hands. White kids smoked, too. It was Heaven at first, all you had to do was scoop the leaves up and roll a dooby. Hell came later.

I wish I'd stayed out of it but I loved smoking dope, I was waving around a cigar-sized blunt. But it wasn't long before a shit-storm exploded through the place. Take sixty kids, pen them up like wild animals month after month, stomp down their every attempt to fight back, and then see what happens when their brains get fired up with monster-strong home-grown weed.

Payback time!! Everybody was screaming, chasing each other, fists flying, bodies slamming. *Crash!*—a double-bunk toppled over onto the floor. I'd never heard such a racket. A window exploded, glass flew like sparks. *Pop-pop-pop!*—light bulbs got smashed along the ceiling. The long room went dark. Flashlights flickered on. Crazed faces glistened with sweat. Eyes glowed out of the rolling smoke. I was still laughing my ass off...then suddenly my heart was whapping inside my chest like a busted fan belt. *Payback Time!* A white kid was being rolled in a blanket, but scrambled away, just barely. I swung myself up on a bunk to look for Mr. Vernon. I couldn't see him anywhere.

A high-pitched shriek cut through the smoke—*"No! Gimme that!"*

It was Fangs, the scrawny kid with the hissing teeth. He always used to carry a black notebook with him, and when anyone threatened him, he'd say "You touch me, I'll write it down!" Pretty lame, but it worked, kids were scared that he'd record what they'd done and pass a notebook page on anonymously to the staff. Now a big guy named Hammer was running down the corridor waving Fangs's book high over his head. Half a dozen other kids were carrying Fangs toward the barracks door. Hammer flung the notebook in the air.

I once heard pigs screaming as their throats were cut, a neighbor of Mr. Vernon came into his pen to do it, and I had to cover my ears, they sounded like babies being sliced open. That was what Fangs's shrieks were like. I found his notebook, ran into the bathroom to open it. Finally, I got to see all the stuff he'd written about everybody!

All I saw in it was page after page of squiggles ≈≈≈≈≈≈≈≈≈ ≈≈≈≈≈≈≈ ≈≈≈≈≈≈≈ ≈≈≈≈≈≈≈ The kid hadn't written anything! Then I remembered how he'd always struggled with the Dick 'n' Jane books in class. The poor little psycho was illiterate!

I spent most of the riot behind a curtain in a bathroom shower stall, squeezing my forehead against the cold tiles, praying that nobody'd think to look there. The grass made me giddy one minute, trembling with terror another. And starving! I wobbled out into the corridor. The barracks door was open. I wandered stupidly out into the parking lot toward the mess hall.

The place was lit up bright as Christmas. A half dozen black kids, including Hammer, were slouched at the tables. Wayne was grinning, smoking a joint. Nobody seemed to notice me. I slipped into a back hall where boxes of food were stored. But the smell wasn't right. It was sickening.

I stopped cold. A kid lay sprawled on the floor. He'd shat his pants, a brown puddle was smeared around him on the cement. His face had been beaten pulpy red like raw hamburger. If it weren't for the hissing sounds he made through his teeth, I couldn't have recognized Fangs. He'd been dumped there in a heap—*payback time.*

As I stood pressed back against the wall, I knew I ought to get my ass out of that place very very fast. Fangs was a bug, whiney and weird, so why should I have given a damn about him? I should have slipped back into the barracks without a word. I'll never know why I didn't.

Instead, I ran gasping from the storage area and out the door.

"*Mr. Vernon! Mr. Vernon! Mr. Vernon!*"

I was still screaming when he found me. He half-fell out of his truck, struggling loose from tangled duct tape. He held me by the shoulders. "What is it, boy? What's happened, son?"

God help me, I told him.

The rest of the night I've just about blocked out. Mr. Vernon must have unlocked the emergency phone's box on the barracks wall to call the troopers. Eventually they came roaring into the camp, red flashers sweeping the grounds. Uniformed thugs in Smokey-the-Bear hats thundered through the building, cracking skulls with nightsticks. Tear-gas canisters flew, their fumes billowed out through the windows. Fangs was rushed off in a wailing ambulance.

But the troopers arrived way too late to help me. The guys in the mess hall had seen me run out calling to Mr. Vernon. The word flash-flooding through the barracks—*Snitch! Snitch!*

Wayne was laughing, yelling the loudest—"*Get him! Blanket party time! Get the snitch!*"

The word still rips into me, spears its way deep into my guts.

Later, the troopers made everyone lie on the gym floor. One by one we were hauled to our feet, plunked down at a desk. One Smokey barked questions, one wrote down our answers.

"Do you know where the marijuana came from?" I was asked.

"I don't know anything about it."

"Where was Mr. Vernon while the disturbance was going on?"

"I don't know."

"How did you get…injured?"

"I don't remember, I was too stoned."

"Who did this terrible thing to you?"

The pain still burned like a red-hot dagger wound. My pants were stuck to the back of my thighs with blood. But I stared straight ahead. "I don't know. I didn't see any faces."

"What *do* you remember?"

"Nothing."

By then, I knew too well what the life expectancy of a snitch was. But for some reason I wanted my life to go on. I didn't know why. Sometimes I still don't. There've been times since that night when I actually wanted to get blown away by enemy gunfire. I still never know when that feeling's going to blaze through me.

The next morning, when I looked in the mirror, my hair had turned grayish white. I got a call to report to the office of the camp's superintendent, a pink-faced prick in a blue shirt. He asked me the same questions the cops had—but in a different way, his eyes focused hard.

"What do you know about what happened?"

"Nothing."

He smiled. *Nothing* was music to his ears.

Then, to see what he'd do, I said, "Well, maybe I do remember *some* things…. "

"No, you don't." His jowls sagged. The smile was gone.

"I don't?"

"Not if you know what's good for you."

"Right." I cocked my head. "And what if I *do* know what's good for me?"

Silence. I heard the clock ticking on his desk. Then he nodded.

So I kept my mouth shut and got my signed discharge papers the very next day.

Onto the bus I went back to New York. Two burly camp social workers beamed smiles at me as I tossed my duffle into the Greyhound's baggage belly.

"Congratulations on your discharge, Pete!"

"Glad you got so much out of our program!"

"Way to go, Pete!"

Way to go.

9

I've bought more supplies—lumber, glass, other materials I need to fix up the house. A lot of my Army disability pay is going, along with my job savings, but it's worth it. The house is filling with furniture, too, but nothing that anyone could see from the road outside. I replace the porch railings at night to make sure nobody drives by and spots me working.

In the office where I sleep, the ceiling and walls are glossy white now, window frames and desk varnished. I love the way the lantern light makes the wood glow. I sit with my feet up. The clouds of spicy smoke from my corncob jolts me back in time to the aroma of turkey stuffing that Laurie and Dolores made once at a Sunday dinner I ate with the family. Mr. Vernon scooped steaming spoonfuls of the stuffing onto our plates. Laurie hummed as she bustled from the kitchen. Dolores sat quietly in a long purple dress, velvety with lace at the neckline. Her black hair seemed to glitter with fireflies in the flicker of candles. Under the table, her bare toe stroked my ankle. She saw me look up at her and smiled.

Tonight I miss them bad, I'm alone more than ever. Sliding open the desk drawer, I hope for more family photos to keep me company. I find newspaper clippings, and come to a picture of Mr. Vernon, those craggy cheeks, stormy white eyebrows, his gaze lowered. That's the way he looked at the dinner table, it's how I've always loved to remember him.

Then I find another clipping.

"No!"

My pipe drops to the floor, sparks exploding from the bowl. I scramble to my feet. I'm sobbing and choking so hard I have to grab the desk to keep from falling.

"No!"

I rush to the front door. The night swells, crickets and frogs and invisible creatures screech up from the grass all around me. It's like I can see myself as they do—not just a scruffy guy standing in a dark doorway but a scrawny kid at the house in Yonkers, watching out the door for my parent who's never coming back.

Now I'm an orphan all over again! The hollow space in my gut aches like a bomb's gone off in it. Finally I shuffle back to the office, still crying, and read the newspaper clipping over and over.

Walter Vernon, 58, local farmer, civic leader, and former NY State Department of Youth Rehabilitation Services employee in Oak Hollow, passed away due to a heart attack in the home of his daughter, Laurinda Vernon, on July 22, 1971. Full obituary and funeral service details will appear in tomorrow's edition.

I rifle the papers in the drawer. No tomorrow's edition, no obituary, no notice of services. But I don't need them. He's been gone *for eleven years!* He died only five days after the riot, four days after I got my discharge papers—7/17/71, all those jagged lines, a date needled on the inside of my skull. I wonder if the riot weakened the old man's heart and he died because he couldn't get to the pills I found under his desk. Or maybe he was so sorrowful no pills could have saved him.

Mr. Vernon went on sick leave right after the camp blew up. I felt awful never getting to say good-bye to him. The night after I reached the halfway house in the city, I sent him a postcard thanking him for everything he'd done for me. The card was the one I'd saved ever since Laurie had bought it for me at the Oak Hill general store a year earlier. It showed trees with glowing orange leaves, a river sparkling in sunshine. I figured it could be a scene from lots of places on his farm. The card was the best treasure I had—which was why I wanted him to have it. I waited and waited for a reply, but none ever came, and I never knew why. Now I do. He must not have lived long enough to get my postcard.

There was so much more I needed to write to him! It would never have fit on a thousand cards. I knew I'd let him down just before the riot. Not fessing up to that has haunted me all my life. It's a big reason I've come back. If he'd returned to the camp, I could have explained to him what happened that night! I needed to—so bad! Would he have forgiven me? Would Laurie have?

The lamp globe's smudged nearly black, the glow's so faint I don't even leave a shadow on the floorboards.

Before the *serape* vanished, I think I believed it had magical qualities that would bring Laurie and Dolores back here. Now that it's gone, I'm not so sure. After reading about Mr. Vernon, I'm too scared to go looking for them right now. Sitting on the daybed, I yank the hunting knife from its sheath that I wear on my belt. I jab the point against my chest as if to poke at the empty hole inside. The blade feels *good* against my skin! I'm not completely empty, there's an aching lump in there. I picture the blade gouging it out—my heart. I heave the heart far out the window all the way to the pond. It sizzles there, sinks deep below the water's surface.

But now I picture Laurie and Dolores coming back, finding me spilling gore all over the floor. I can't do that to them!

I have to clean the sooty lantern globe, stop all the flickering. The house brightens just enough. I start scraping the walls in the parlor to get them ready for a layer of primer. The dawn bleaches the sky behind the barn. I scrape and scrape until my arm won't rise one more time. I drop onto the bed. When I wake up it's afternoon, maybe the beginning of evening.

— *Wow, Slick, I can't believe what you've done in here!*

— *The walls are so clean, Pedro, the ceiling—it looks like Heaven!*

I get back to work.

How long have I been in the house? Maybe a couple of weeks, maybe more. The house—and me, probably, we seem to be the same thing—smells of detergent, paint, fresh wood shavings. It echoes with hammer racket, saw rasping, the high-pitched song of a sanding machine I've attached to my car battery. Most of the rooms are scraped and painted, two coats downstairs, and I've replaced the rails and rotted boards on the porch. Most of the windows have new frames and glass, I've put new hinges on the front door, a shiny brass latch and knocker. I listen for that knocker to clack, sometimes hopefully, sometimes in dread, but I'm glad it's there.

In the basement I find the heavy old scythe. It's still pretty sharp. The first time I tried to swing it, I nearly flung myself over in the grass. Cracking a big smile, Mr. Vernon held me steady, the way a baseball coach helps a rookie get his swing right. "There's a natural rhythm to it, just like everything else," he said. "Once you learn, you can keep on without thinking about it."

I sort of knew what he meant. I'd seen a few guys who could go through life like that—pick up a rhythm easy and then just move along with it. They got good grades, made the team, met the pretty girls, went off to college. I seemed to have been born without that rhythm. Yet Mr. Vernon thought I could find it. When he moved my arm with his hands, the scythe's swing felt effortless, right. "Nice and smooth. No need to swipe so hard at the grass. Just let the blade scoop it up," he said. So I swung my arms with the long curved blade making wide smiles through the grass, and pretty soon I was walking along slowly…swing… swing …swing…and the grass was sweeping aside for me in long green waves. I'd learned the rhythm!

When I try to scythe the grass around the house now, I stumble at first, nicking my shins, and pretty soon a fierce muscle ache grabs my shoulder. I slow down my swing. *Slow…slow….* After a while I'm making a wider path as I move. Easy…smooth….. The rhythm's back! I wish Laurie and Dolores would drive up and see me now!

In the town, when I pass the graveyard, I stop beside the angels to tell them how I'm fixing up the house. Sometimes I get the chills talking to them, worrying that maybe Laurie and Dolores are angels, too, now—no wonder I'm dragging my feet looking for them! But usually I just like checking in with the ladies in their shapely stone robes.

"The grass is so short now I can see the pond from the office window," I tell them.

How does it look?

"Silvery. And I bought some aluminum chairs to put around it, and some for the parlor."

How does the parlor look?

"The floor still needs some more sanding. But the walls, the ceiling—they look good!"

You like to make the work last as long as you can, don't you?

"Maybe." I glace away. "Yeah, I do."

Well, there's no hurry.

Stay as long as you like.

You're always welcome here.

"But what about finding Laurie and Dolores?"

Silence.

"Why don't they come back?"

Silence.

"Where are they?"

The wind rustles the leaves in the trees, then fades.

I finally get up the nerve to look for Mr. Vernon's grave. The rounded headstone's in a corner next his wife's. Has anyone been here to clean it? I can't tell, the stone looks so pocked, weathered. I try to talk to the old man, but words turn to ashes in my throat. Eyes stinging wet, I scrub his head-stone with a brush from the car. Then his wife's. Years of gunk have stuck in the indented letters. I dig them out with my knife point, scraping each letter clean. With my fingers I rake leaves away from the stones' bases so the tiny green blades of grass show. Slowly I back off.

Near the obelisk, Lance's square marker's been tended, probably by some Legion vets, with five little flags poked up at angles. I straighten them in a row and give Lance a sharp shine-up so I can see my reflection in the smooth marble.

At a place down the main road, I buy a propane cylinder and hook up the kitchen stove. The first time I light a match, I squinch my eyes tight, picturing the kitchen exploding like in a grenade detonation. But *piff!*–circles of low blue flames shoot up. No more cheese sandwiches and cold beans from the can. I've bought pork chops and potatoes and carrots. I cook my first meal here in my new pans, sit at my new table to eat. I want to tell the angels about this…but I think I know what they'd say.

The house is starting to look like it did, Pete.
But how much longer can you stay here alone?

10

I wear a white t-shirt, jeans, shitkicker boots—my new slouter disguise—and sure enough, the Deer's Head Tavern is full of guys dressed like me, nobody even blinks in my direction when I step inside. A familiar funk of beer suds tugs me toward the back room where drinkers curl over tables in the dark, snails in a hollow log. But I stay in the front where the neon blinks. I haven't touched any alcohol for twenty-five months, but it wasn't my biggest problem, and if I have just a few bottles of Bud—what all the country boys have clamped like gearshift knobs in their fists—I'll probably be okay. Or not. But I got to risk it tonight.

Sitting in a booth, I try to spot some older guys who might remember farm people from eleven years ago. The bartender looks like he might have ridden a few tractors in his day— close-cropped head, beefy arms, big hands reaching out to serve customers and scoop up bills. On an electric beer sign behind the bar, blue river-light ripples over plastic rocks and over him, too, like he's treading water. Balls clack on a pool table, men chalk their cues and lean over like sharpshooters. Tammy Wynette's trapped behind the pink glass of the jukebox, squealing to be let out. No "Me and Bobby Mcgee." Well, shit, it's years later and I'm practically an old fart in here, except I'm as ripped as any of the guys I see. I don't worry about them trying to take me down, I've survived fights in dives that make this one look like a day care center. That's not what I'm nervous about.

Some girls drift around, lots of raccoon eyes and pillowy lips and sparkly do-dads dangling from earlobes. Most find guys in feed caps to snuggle up to. A Lone Rangerette in a cowboy hat swings herself down into my booth. I can't see much of her face, the way she's got the hat brim tilted. She's jiggling her leg so hard I feel the table vibrating.

"Hey, you speak English?" She leans toward me.

I try to smile but my skin feels so tight it hurts "It's been a while." I say.

"You sure look like it has!" Her voice is ragged around the edges. "How come?"

None of your fucking business! I almost say it, but press the lip of my beer bottle hard against my bottom lip. *Ask her about Laurie! Go on—ask her!....* Too late—she's seen my scowl and weaves away from the booth. Suddenly I'm sorry.

After all, I found Raquel in a bar, too. She was trolling drunks for drug money and I had to half-carry her to the rehab center kicking and thrashing; her elbow cracked one of my teeth, but it was worth it. Calming down, she sang in her high, laughing voice, "I ain't heavy I'm your sister," a takeoff on the line in the war song— "He ain't heavy he's my brother," a song I loved a lot. At first, in the group therapy program I ran, she talked like I *was* her big brother, and I ate that up. Hardly nobody'd ever looked *up* to me in my life, usually it was the other direction. Raquel was on the plump side, with a dark pretty face, big glowing eyes and hair like black satin feathers all over her shoulders. I never met anybody who trusted me the way she did, so I was nervous about coming on to her. But she didn't mind fumbling with me in bed, she had a mission to help me perk up, the way I had a mission to help her stay clean. Now we were more equal. That made all our efforts sweet, no matter if they ended with me squirting into her palm or up against cheek, she just laughed and pushed my head down towards her pussy, "My turn, Petey." She was the only woman who ever called me that. And when we finally had our mission-accomplished celebrations, *"Petey!"* was the name she cried in my ear. I loved to listen to her whisper it as she lay her head on my chest. The shadow of the fire escape slowly climbed the wall as the sun sank outside the window. I thought I'd finished my counseling job with her, but I should have known better, no matter how calm she seemed and how fine she made me feel.

People start to leave the tavern and now I can crowd my way to the bar where the guy behind it leans on his elbows. I saddle up a stool and order a second beer. "Forgot what pretty country it is around here," I say. "I'd love to bring my wife, show her these mountains."

He just nods. No smile.

"I'm staying with folks I used to visit a lot when I was a teenager."

He wipes the bar down with a rag.

"Buy you one?" I ask.

"Nope." He shoots some soda from the backstage hose into a glass. An AA shot.

His khaki shirt and the camouflage pants make me nervous. It's hard to keep myself from psyching out guys to see if they're vets—even though brings it brings up memories of things I did in Vietnam that got me suicide watches in the stockade and mandatory shrink visits. But also a medical discharge with disability benefits. I keep my eyes on the bartender's rag as he rubs it hard on the polished wood like he's trying to scrub off invisible spots. Yeah, he's a vet. And he cops to it. After another couple beers, I'm spouting some tales about Saigon I haven't told for years.

"Hey, sorry—I'm Rob." I grin again at the bartender. Where'd I get "Rob?" Short for Robinson Crusoe? "What's your name?" I ask.

"Billy." He looks at his watch. It's an hour til closing time.

"You know, I remember a family named Vernon lived around here," I say. "Nice people. Had a farm. You ever hear of them?"

"Mm."

"I heard what happened to Mr. Vernon. Awful thing. Heart attack, I guess."

"Yeah."

I nod. "He worked part-time for the state, I think. Some kind of reform school place they used to have up in the woods?"

"Yeah, the state camp. It's shut down now."

"Did you…." I clear my throat. "Did you ever know Mr. Vernon's daughter, Laurie?"

"The Vernons lived over to Oak Hollow. I'm from Middleburg, myself."

"Laurie was a pistol, I guess."

"Some said that."

I lean forward. "What happened to her?"

He scratches his cheek. I hear a rustle of clothing nearby. The cowgirl's back. She's got bright eyes but lots of deep lines fan out beside them. She could be 25, could be 55. I hope to hell she's not going to sit with us, just as I've worked the conversation here around to Laurie. *Shit!* She parks herself on the stool beside mine and waves at Billy, a circular flat-palmed movement like somebody erasing a blackboard.

"Hit me again?" She points to a bottle behind him on the shelf.

"Last one ain't paid for, Paula."

I feel her eyes poking me and stare at the rippling waterfall sign. We're all treading water in here. Paula fumbles in her purse, fishes out coins. They scatter on the shiny surface of the bar. Her long silver fingernails make her clumsy. "I got more in here, I know I do!"

"Never mind." I push a five dollar bill toward Billy.

He splashes some vodka into a glass, slides it to her. "Last call for you, Paula."

"Show some fuckin respect for a lady," she says. "I ain't in no bad condition."

"So anyway...." I turn back to Billy. "Laurie?"

He wipes the bar with his rag again. "I heard she took off down south after her dad passed."

"Did she ever come back here?"

Billy shrugs and steps far back. Suddenly I know he doesn't mean to tell me anything more.

Paula leans toward me. "What d'you want to know 'bout Laurie for?"

My head snaps sideways. "Just wondering," I say. "She's sort of like...an old friend."

"I 'member hearing about her." Paula gazes at me over the top of her glass, eyelashes nearly stuck together with mascara, pupils dilated. "First of all, she goddamn near got *run out* of here after her dad passed, she didn't just *leave*."

I frown. "What happened?"

"Things I could tell you, maybe…."

I catch a glimpse of Billy rolling his eyes as he turns away.

"Is Laurie still around?" I ask Paula.

From her purse she pulls out a pack of cigarettes and clacks the lighter down on the bar in front of me. "You can light my fire," she says.

On the dirt turnaround behind the tavern, Paula's car, a Japanese rust-bucket, is parked in shadows under some branches away from the building's neon glow. The car smells like something sticky-sweet and familiar. Paula reaches across me, opens the glove compartment. Out comes her hand holding what I can see even in this shadowy light is a glass pipe. *Oh shit!*

"It can get lonesome out in the country." She drops her head onto my shoulder, letting the cowboy hat tumble to the floor. The pipe rises in her hand in front of my face. "I could tell, you were a guy who likes to get high…."

It *still* shows? "Uh huh…."

"Don't you just wish this thing was loaded?"

I feel a trembling in my eyelids, my fingertips. The times I've smoked crack in my life were so incredibly good—full-body orgasms! Then I remember the guys in my meetings who ranted on about how the smoke made their eyes melt like grilled gumdrops, how their pipes cried out to them and turned them into predatory beasts of the night. A breeze blows through my window, and I hear leaves rustling, rustling, like whispers.

"Listen, Paula--you tell me about Laurie," I say. "Then we can think about scoring."

"Thing is, I got a problem." She sighs. "This family court judge, he took my daughter away from me. She's with my sister in Ohio. I'm gonna need some travelling money to go see her."

"I'll do what I can, Paula."

She leans her head farther back. "Gonna need two new tires...."

"Okay."

"I sure miss my little girl...."

Why am I listening to this junkie con? Well, because...I remember the urgent, tearful voice of Raquel...then recall my own wheedling voice, too.... Leaning forward, I yank my wallet from my back pocket.

Her eyes widen, focusing on two twenties I lay on her knee. She turns slowly to me. "Them tires really going to cost me."

I lay down another twenty, put my wallet away. "Tell me about Laurie."

Paula takes a deep breath. "Well, after her old man passed...must've been ten, eleven years ago...."

"Eleven."

"Whatever. She left town fast, Laurie did. Tried to get into the music business down in Texas, but I heard they didn't go for her hotshot act there. Folks had her figured for a commie war-protester. Same as they did here." Paula shakes her head slowly. "Laurie hadn't ought to of come back."

"She's *back?*"

"About a month ago she turned up. Big and brassy as ever."

"Listen, did her friend come with her? Dolores?"

"I don't know about no…Dolores. I didn't hear." Paula shrugs. "Alls I know is, Laurie went to some lawyers in Albany, sold most of the land her old man left her."

"What did she do with it?"

"Well, she bought the old Glen Castle Hotel."

"*That* place?" I lean forward. "Hey, is she living there?"

Paula folds the bills in her lap. "I 'spect she's there now."

I ram my shoulder against the car door and lurch out into the darkness.

11

Driving back, I somehow get lost in a maze of dirt roads. They turn, they stop, they fade into tracks that narrow into underbrush. I back up, try other turns. My wrists hurt as I yank the steering wheel from side to side. Barns appear in my headlight beams, stone walls march off into dark woods. In the moonlight, a rusted hay-rake sprawls in a field like the rib-cage of a brontosaurus. My tires roll into a rut. I hit the brakes hard. The car bumps sideway, its radiator burrowed into a deep field.

I shift in reverse, back through whining mud to the road, and ram the car into drive. On and on I bump. Finally I come out of the maze onto a paved road, and find my way back to the house.

The next morning, I'm too nervous to head out to the hotel yet, and sit on the side porch in one of the three rocking chairs I bought down the road at a flea market. As I rock, I feel the floorboards gradually tilting me toward the edge. The sun's glow relaxes my face, and I start thinking about what it might be like to see Dolores again. It seems like just last week when she was here on this porch with me. She and I sat side by side in rockers while Laurie

94

Slick

went off with her father to get the tractor repaired in the next town. If Mr. Vernon forgot to give me a chore while he went away, Laurie always did, but today she hadn't said a word to me when she drove off.

As Delores and I rocked, she found one cigarette left in the crumpled pack of Luckies she took from her skirt pocket. She lit it and passed it to me before she even took a real drag, herself. The evening sizzle of bugs was just starting in the fields. Waves of high grass rippled across the road. She was watching me, those narrow "Cheena" eyes bright, her mouth poised to grin, like she expected me to do some magic trick. So I did, just a routine that incarcerated guys spend months learning, to kill time—rolling a lit cigarette in and out through my fingers.

She laughed and clapped her hands. "Pedro the magician!"

Our rockers creaked slowly. "What's it like in Mexico?" I asked her. I'd always wanted to know about where she came from.

She wrinkled her nose. "More poor than here."

"You still like to wear the clothes, though," I said. She had on a blue cotton blouse with tiny red peppers sewn around the low neckline. I always noticed what she was wearing, she took more care about her outfits than Laurie did. "So you must miss it, at least a little."

"Oh, *yes!*" When she smiled, lines shot from the sides of her eyes. They weren't age lines, she was only 19, a teenager like me—which I'd just found out recently, it blew my mind. "I think about my village sometimes." She leaned far back as if to get a better view of it in the distance. "My family lived near the ocean. I could hear the waves splash. And smell the salt in the air." She closed

95

her eyes. "But I don' talk so much about Mexico. Laurie don' like to hear about it…."

"How come?"

"I think she is escared I will go back." Dolores sighed. "She worries I will get sad here when her father drinks too much and talks about her brother. You always say this farmhouse is so cheer-ful, and it is—especially whenever you come. But sometimes, is a dark kind of place."

"I didn't know that." I hand her the cigarette.

She stares at the glowing end. "Sometimes Laurie goes out at night by herself, she knows the 'gin mills.' They are too rough for me, she says. So I stay alone in the house with the dark. All I do is I practice my songs, my guitar, try to fill up the quiet. Sometimes she don' come back till morning. Then she is hard with me, push me down on the bed, crying and—" Dolores made clawing movements with her bent fingers. "After, she is sorry, sorry, sorry. She tells me Don' do this chore, that chore— jus' rest. But if I don' work, what am I going to do here?"

"Cook tacos and enchiladas?"

She turned slowly to me, blinking hard like that would help bring back her smile.

"And brownies?" I rock a little faster.

"I eat too many brownies these days." Smiling now, she patted her belly. It was a little rounder than before, but I liked the soft shape of it under her pale cotton skirt. Then she rolled her eyes, fluttering her hand up past her face like a wisp of smoke. "I ate a strong brownie jus' a while ago—whew!" Now her smile was back. "I can get one for you if you wan'."

"Sure—great. But finish what you were saying."

She settled farther back in her chair. "In Mexico, my father got in trouble selling mari-huana. The big man in the village, he wanted to be the only one who was selling it. He had guns, said he gonna rape me. My father, he was always locking me inside. He got so escared for me he paid a *coyote* to take me across the border to Texas. I went to live with my cousins, but they don' got money to feed me. They jus' throw me out." Dolores took a long drag on the cigarette. "That was when Laurie foun' me. She saved me. Taught me English, bought me food, clothes, everything. So now I don' like to worry her. She got enough to upset her…." Dolores sighed. "She don' need to cry about me leaving her. I tell her so many times—I can never go back to Mexico."

"Why not?"

"You are always so curious about everything!" She smiled. "People here say that it kills the cats. But I don' believe that. Do you?"

"Only sometimes." At the camp, I stayed blind and deaf, that was how I survived. But I could never hear enough of Dolores's and Laurie's and Mr. Vernon's stories. They helped fill the huge holes in my own story, if I even had one. I'd never heard Dolores talk so much. This was the first time we'd been together, just the two of us. "So why won't you go back to Mexico?" I asked.

Dolores rocked faster. "You know, my father's job, he cut sugar cane. Is the worse job in the worl'. My mother had to tie up his hands with wet cloths, they have so many blisters, burns, cuts. But then he got drunk on cactus liquor and beat her with the same hands. I hated so much to see it, hear her scream!"

"I know something about that," I said finally.

"Your father did this, too?" She turned to me. I could see her focus wavering, her eyes dilated.

"Yeah. If I wasn't there when it happened, she filled me in on the gory details. He knocked me around, too, when I made too much noise. She thought it was *her* fault when he pounded on me. And on *her,* too."

"Thas not right."

"Then—it was my fault he left us, she'd say. Unless it was hers."

"No, thas all *loco!*" Dolores spun one finger in a circle beside her head.

I nodded. "She couldn't help being like she was. Once time she smacked my fourth grade teacher over the head with a glass flower vase. Because the guy'd been picking on me. So I was kind of proud of her, even when the security guards dragged her out of the classroom."

Dolores pressed her fingers over her mouth, smiling at me over them. Then her look faded, and she dropped her hand. "When I couldn' remember what my teachers taught, they slapped me. Is why I stopped school. I was only esmall."

I reached out to slow Dolores's chair so she wouldn't tip it over. "What grade?"

She sighed. "I only got two years in school. Thas all."

A few weeks before, I'd told her about *Treasure Island,* a book one of the camp teachers had loaned me. No wonder she kept asking to hear more about it, she'd probably never read any books in her life. If I hadn't been able to read at the camp library and find books at other juvey detention places I'd been, I'd have gone mad. What would it be like if you couldn't have any other place to go in your mind except where you actually had to be? How could anybody stand that?

I wanted to cheer Dolores up, so I asked her about good times she'd had with her family. Then she did remember some things she hadn't thought of in years. I loved the way her eyes sparkled again. At Christmas time, she said, her grandparents always hung up a *piñata*, a bull made from colored paper. The kids hit it with sticks so lots of little presents fell out. Once she got a shiny starling made of flattened tin. She still had it.

"Is that the bird on your guitar? The blue one?"

"You saw it!" She smiled. "*Yes!* I glued it on, for good luck."

She reached out sideways as she rocked, her hand on my arm again. Our feet rested side by side on the porch railing. She was wearing gold plastic sandals, I could see her purple toenails wiggling inside them. The chairs creaked faintly in unison. She watched me, her eyelashes blinking slowly. The buzzing from the grass swelled in my ears.

"So rough, your skin feels," she murmured. "You do so much work here!"

"I can't get enough of it." We'd almost stopped rocking now. I slowly raised my hand and stroked the side of her neck. Her hair fell silky across my knuckles. She took my hand and moved it down her shoulder. My fingers slipped under the light cotton of her blouse. I half-closed my eyes. Now I was holding her breast in the palm of my hand like it was a warm baby bird.

We rocked together in time with our breathing. Her eyes shut. I felt dozy myself. Then she lifted my hand and placed it on the arm of my chair. "I promised I will get you brownies. You wan' lemonade, too?"

On our way to the kitchen, I watched the way her skirt swayed, the curve of her hips tight in the soft cotton. She seemed to forget where she was going, pausing to gaze at the oil paintings on the wall. I stood beside her to look over some mountains and valleys of golden wheat—scenes not so different from ones we could often see from the fields higher on the farm. In one painting, naked ladies were splashing in a lake while goats grazed nearby, their eyes twinkly like they were sneaking sideways glances.

"What are you thinking?" I whispered to Dolores. She seemed to have floated into the painting.

Her shoulders squirmed, shifting her dark curls. "The goats are smiling."

"That's what I thought, too."

She laughed and turned toward the kitchen again. I walked a little behind her. She gazed at the stairs and paused on the carpet beside the railing. My arms seemed to rise on their own, and then I was wrapping them around her. She pressed her cheek against my chest. I smelled her sweet, sweaty scent. Shutting my eyes, I held her close.

12

Bong!

We jumped apart.

Bong!

It was just the tall grandfather clock in the corner. Its vibrations hung in the air— *two...o'clock....* The chill on the back of my neck faded, turned to a warm glow again.

Dolores raised her face. I kissed her, my lips pressing against the corner of her mouth. Then she gripped me tight. Our lips moved together, her tongue twitched like a crazy little fish waiting for me. We were gobbling each other up, a couple of starving children.

In her room the air smelled as if the wallpaper roses were giving off pollen. When we sprawled onto her soft quilt, the mattress let out a laughing squeak. I was about to fling myself onto her but she rolled into a ball, pressing her forehead against my shoulder.

"Pedro, please don' be rough with me!"

I didn't really know what else to do with girls, my sex life up to then had been wrestling matches on friends' basement mattresses. Suddenly I didn't want to fuck Dolores, I wanted to protect her, rescue her, wrap myself around her to keep all the goats and thugs like me from

101

hurting her. When I did hold her, she was trembling. She wiped her damp cheek against my arm.

Then I had a scary thought and stared at her wristwatch. "What time are Laurie and the old man coming back?"

"Four o'clock, Laurie tol' me." Dolores unbuckled the watch. She set it down on the bedside table behind the base of a china lamp, its face turned away from us. I was sure it had been a present from Laurie.

"Slow, slow" she whispered.

She wasn't spooked now, just eager to get to know every part of me she touched. She wanted to feel the way my fingers and lips felt against her skin before I moved farther along her body. The breeze from the open window blew across my back and billowed the gauzy blue curtains over the bed.

She glanced at them. "Like feathers!"

"Your bird wings," I whispered.

She pressed my arm against hers, smiling at the paleness of my skin against the gold of her own. I hoped it would rub off on me, gold dust, caramel dust we could both taste. She was amazed by the hair curling around my nipples, she had no idea what they were for. "To rub against you." I told her as she brushed her lips over my chest. I remembered the way her breasts had bounced in the air when she'd sung her song standing on the truck cab's roof, and now they couldn't stop bobbing and heaving high in the air when she arched her back. She clamped her hand over mine when I pressed my fingers over her pussy, rocking her hips and squeezing her legs together. Suddenly she went tense and quivered all over, letting out a little squeal. I pushed my face into her hair. Drunk on its scent, I brushed my lips down her neck.

My cock seemed to amaze her—its color, it's blue veins, the little "eye" at the end. "Why you're crying like that?" She asked it, looking close.

"Just happy." I wiggled it, Pedro the Magician.

She held me in her fist, running one finger over the tiny drop of clear fluid. Tasting it with her tongue, she wrinkled her nose, giggling. Then she lay her cheek on my belly, exploring my balls—"so wrinkly, so many curls."

"Not as many as you got, I said," which was true, her bush was thick and black. She spread her legs a little to look and compare, and I wanted to dive in face-first, something forbidden I'd always wanted to try. But suddenly my cock went off in her fist.

"Oh God!" she sat back quickly.

"Don't let go!" I gasped.

"Is like milk from—" Her fingers made the squeezing movement that I'd been taught to make on a cow's udder. My cock drooped sideways. "Did I hold it too hard?" she asked.

"It'll be back. We'll just have to figure out things to do while we wait."

She snuggled tight against me. We held each other every way we could think of. Face to face with limbs twining like a couple of squirmy octopuses. Back to front, curling together like spoons. When we lay together upside down, I got to satisfy my curiosity about the furry, warm anemone that lived in her bush. She pushed it against my mouth, up and down, her thighs clamping my cheeks til I gasped, dizzy for air.

We lay back, our heads on the pillows. Her smile faded as I finally lay on top of her, propping myself up on one elbow to keep from crushing her. I pushed inside her. She stared up at me, a shocked look on her face.

I almost pulled out. "Does it hurt?" I whispered.

"No, no." She gasped. "You feel so big. Hurry—"

And so I did, losing myself in her and finally collapsing with a gasp on her shoulder. She hadn't moved much beneath me, but she was soft and welcoming now, holding my sides gently with her knees, stroking my hair.

"I made you happy?" she whispered.

"Mmm-hm. You?"

"Jus' stay with me, like this."

And I would have happily stayed forever, my cheek resting on her chest, my heart slowly thumping in time with hers.

She dug her fingers into my scalp. "You were esleeping." She kissed my nose. "You din' even hear the bong-bong-bongs. The father clock, downstairs."

I sat up fast. "What time is it?"

"Only three. Like the clock said." She stroked my shoulder. My heart was drumming now, I had to press my fist hard against my chest.

"I thought Mr. Vernon was coming back." I pictured the old man climbing the stairs, calling my name, his face craggy and hard. "He trusts me in his house. I can't make him mad at me—"

"Nobody is mad." Dolores ran her finger along my cheek. "Don't cry, Pedro!"

"I'm not!" But I was. I sniffled hard. "But yeah, you're right, we still got time."

"We din' do nothin' bad!"

"No, that's right. I loved it. But...." I shut my eyes tight.

"Maybe Laurie could get angry a little." Dolores shrugged. "But who knows who *she* goes with—in the gin mills? I don' fight with her about that, so she can not fight with me. Anyway, she won' know. So she don' get hurt or angry. Nobody is going to know, right?"

"Right." I lay down beside her again. "I promise."

Between long gusts of breeze the whole house seemed to hum with heat. I noticed the sun-faded wallpaper again with columns of roses twining up and up. A poster of her favorite women singer was tacked up beside the bed. A shiny belt hung from a hook on the frame of a cave-like closet. Several skirts and blouses were flung over a chair—red, orange, blue—and I wanted to see her wearing each outfit, turning this way and that in the full-length mirror, flinging her arms in the air like a dancer to show off the colors to me. Girl-mysteries were everywhere—strange scents I ached to breathe in deeper, silky textures I needed to stroke. A guitar lay glossy and woman-shaped in a bedlike case of deep blue velvet. I longed to see Dolores sit strumming the strings, hear her voice flutter around the room.

The bed squeaked, Dolores stood up. I'd never seen anyone so lovely in my life—the shapes of her round belly, her quivering breasts. Then she was covering all that golden skin with her skirt and blouse. I got to my feet, too, reaching for my clothes.

"We should go down." She glanced toward the door and the stairwell.

"We better." I buckled my belt. Then I wrapped my arms around her.

She rubbed her forehead against my chest. "Life is so happy here—mos' of the time. And I love Laurie so much, and her father, and this farm. It was good here before—

the garden, the music, the house. But when you came to work, it was like you'd always belonged. Our life changed so much better! So much! I don' know how to say…."

"I love you all, too." My voice came out in a whisper.

"So we got to be careful we don' spoil everything here, Pedro!"

"I know!" My heart slammed. "I don't want you to get hurt, Dolores."

"Or you." She touched my cheek.

"If Mr. Vernon knew, he'd think I'd betrayed his trust. I couldn't stand that!"

"I know. I couldn' either." She sighed. "Is too much risk…if we do this another time."

"That's so sad!"

She nodded slowly.

"But I'm sort of…relieved, too," I said.

She touched her chest. "Yes, both. They hurt, don' they?"

"Yeah…." I felt the ache in my chest, too. We shared it. We'd always share it.

Now there's only one chair on this porch, at least for now. I jump up and hurry inside to the office to make sure the tin bird's still dangling on its chain from the rifle peg. It's there, shiny blue beside the open window. I lie on my back on the bed, hold it above my face, try to imagine hanging the chain around Dolores's neck. But she's blurring into Raquel now. I used to buy Raquel chains with pendants, she loved them, especially with sparkly stones. I miss both girls so much! When I find Dolores, will it seem like Raquel's come back, too?

I need to work some more, keep busy, make the house beautiful for Dolores, for Laurie—for the old man, too—make it like they've remembered it.   I've started painting some window frames out back where they can't be seen from the road. I painted with Laurie and her old man years ago, all of us spattered with white freckles— jeans, work shirts, even our hair. "You look like an albino leopard, Dad," Laurie told him. "Doesn't he, Slick?" And I nodded. He chuckled. I loved the way she got me to help her joke him out of his dark moods. She and him were a team, running the farm together. And I was on the team. They both figured I could do any job if they just showed me how, and since they believed it, I could.

I work until dark, and lie down on the office bed for a short snooze. In a while I hear an engine growl faintly down the road. Shit—I left the rocker on the porch! I race to the door, drag the chair inside across the boards just as headlights flicker at the edge of the field. Squatting down, I peer around the door frame. It's the Crown Vic, its twin antennae-beams probing the room, splashing white against the walls. The rocker's shadow lengthens along the floor. I squat lower so as not to cast a shadow, myself. The car sweeps by, its tires crunching dirt. Then the walls fall backwards and the room goes dark again. The engine sound fades…dissolves into the night.

13

This morning I roll down to the main road before I have a chance to delay myself any longer with a saw or paint brush or daydreams. At the truck stop I get a hot shower, then stuff my filthy clothes into a machine at the laundromat next door. I sit on a bench reading *Crime and Punishment* while my clothes clunk around, and who should walk in but Bartender Billy? He eyeballs me but turns away when I nod. Maybe I'm wearing out my welcome in this area? Fuck it, I can't wear out what I haven't got. In clean blue jeans and a fresh white t-shirt, I toss the other clothes into the Caddie's trunk and head out.

In Oak Hollow, I spot the wings of the angels rising above the cemetery wall, and stop the car and step out onto the grass.

"Hey, ladies—I made it back!"

And you found out what you wanted to know, one of them whispers.

So what are you doing back here now? the other one asks.

"That old hotel—I'm sort of spooked to go there." I feel the ladies stare at me out of their blank stone all-seeing eyes. "After all these years, I've wanted so bad to come back, but now that I'm so close…."

You don't have to rush.

Wait a while.

You can stay with us.

Lie down in the grass.

Just close your eyes, sink into the ground….

I blink hard, sure I hear faint laughter. "No, I can't stay here any longer!" I rush back to the car. The engine's still idling.

Take care, Pete!

Good luck!

Good luck, Pete!

"So long, ladies!" Waving through the open window, I drive away.

My fingers grip the wheel, my spine's locked in a forward tilt. The tires sing off-key. Around a bend…and there's the hotel! The place has been so bleached by sunlight that it looks as cloud-white as I remember it from eleven years ago. I hope I'll find the shutters open, glowing like magic wings…but up close, the place appears just as shut tight and gloom-soaked as it did when I last passed it. I roll through bumper-high grass and brake on a bald patch by the main door.

The door's still locked. *Shit!* I knock and knock and knock, wait on tiptoe. Silence. I bash the wood with both fists, tears stinging my eyes.

"*Laurie! Dolores! Let me in!*" I picture the girls huddling together as the racket echoes inside. "*It's me, Pete!--*" An awful picture: two skeletons in decayed rags lean over the bar, skulls turn toward the door. *"Please!—"* The cry feels like ground glass in my throat.

I stagger away from the door, roar off in the car, eyes dangerously blurred. Nothing but static on the radio but I crank it up anyway, anything to sandblast my mind. Where do I drive all day? I don't know, but it's not the highway north to Montreal—not yet, not yet. The sky turns greenish gray, maybe a storm coming in. Eerie how the twilight birds have all gone silent at once. I shoot back toward the town.

Thunder booms overhead. Then rain is splashing so hard against my windshield I have to slow to a crawl. Silver waves streaks down the glass. I'm gliding half-blind through deeper waters than I've ever seen before. Jagged tree branches echo lightening flashes overhead. Now a heavy fog blurs the road. I drive on, creeping along a murky ocean floor. Finally the outline of hotel appears up ahead, a castle of white coral....

And look! The first-floor lights—*they're glowing!* The building floats in iridescent gauze—tall walls and turrets and steep-sloping roofs. I brake too fast and seem to skid *upwards*—like I'm surfacing from out of the deep. The car whirls off the asphalt, fishtailing—slides to a halt in high grass. I've lost all sense of direction.

As I open the car door a flying barrage of water soaks me—hair, clothes, skin. The hotel's gone. Was I hallucinating it? I'm so dizzy I have to lean over and press my fingertips into the puddled ground. *Breathe...slow....* Finally I stand straight. And turn around—

The hotel's back—behind me! Its windows flicker behind the fog and gusts of rain. My car's fins have come to rest inches from the hood of a pick-up truck parked in the spattering mud. A few yards away is the hotel's door. The knob's shinier than I remember it. It turns easy now.

The door swings open into a big room that's edged in such deep shadows that it seems to have no walls. I make out a stocky, spike-haired figure standing behind a long bar in front of a row of wall lamps. Their glare makes me squint. I pull the door shut behind me. *Click.* A hush falls over the wide space between me and the person. I smell bitter coffee. The figure doesn't move. I can't see the shadowy face. But whoever's there can see me. I know I'm being looked over.

"Laurie?" My voice sounds faint in here. "Hey—*Laurie?*"

Rain ticks against the French doors' glass. I sway in place.

A familiar, brassy voice— "Well, Slick, I wondered when you'd turn up!"

Of course it's Laurie!   She's been waiting for me! "Yeah...I'm back!" I wipe my wet face with my sleeve, step closer.

Laurie steps sideways, and now light falls over her-- cheeks round and splotchy, lips pressed together, eyes deep-set and slanted down at the outer corners like she's about to burst into tears or maybe into roars of laughter. Where's the pulled-back hair, the braid dangling down her back? Gone—her hair's chopped off, bristly. I see wide colored stripes—the *serape* she's wearing. She *was* the one who took it from the house! The material's loose over her shoulders, the fringe dangles.

"*Laurie!*"

"Yep." She rests her elbows on the bar, shoulders hunched forward. Those deep lines around her eyes shock me—she can't have grown that old! She picks up a coffee mug, watches me over its rim. "You came back. Like a bad penny."

I clear my throat. "Only a penny?"

"Just an expression. Don't know why I thought of it," she says. "What the hell happened to your hair? You see a ghost somewhere?"

"It just…changed color. A long time ago."

"They told me it was freaky white but—"

"*Who* told you? How'd you know I was coming?"

She tilts her head, I think she's enjoying my puzzlement. "Well, I got the crazy letter you wrote to my father. Someone from the PO shoved it under the door here a while ago."

"Damn, it got here after I did. You thought it was crazy?" I don't wait for an answer. "I was in a wild mood when I wrote it, I guess."

"You could say that, yeah…." She steps back. "Anyway, Billy phoned me about you from the Deer's Head. And again today. Must've been half a dozen folks called me lately, said some scruffy guy with a pointy-assed car was living in my old house. I still own it, you know."

"I only saw a few cars go past. Nobody stopped." I frown. "Does one of your friends drive a long, black Crown Vic?"

"Sure," she says. "The deputy sheriff."

"Oh, shit!"

"You think you could hole up at that house and nobody'd notice? In *this* town?" She reaches under the bar, sets out another mug and a glass pot of coffee. "Want some?"

"Yeah!" This is more like it! I start toward her, glancing around the room. The floor gleams like black ice, goes back on and on into the shadows. Laurie must have polished the bar counter, I can smell new varnish. The dark wood reflects a row of globes in shiny brass fixtures behind the bar, they're below the wall-length mirror that I remember from the afternoon concert Laurie and Dolores gave here. The glass seems to have water trickling down it, but that's just the reflected rain falling outside the windows. The rain smells fresh, even in here. Now I see the far wall, but where are the murals of shepherdesses? Painted over years ago, probably. The chandeliers have been amputated, nothing left of them but stumps poking down from the ceiling.

"You can pull up a seat," Laurie says, her voice like a sigh, like she's been waiting for me behind that counter for so long that actually seeing me again has lost any surprise, and now I'm just sort of inevitable.

"This is your place, now, huh?" I sit on a high stool. It feels rickety, precarious.

"My domain. Far as the eye can see." She fills a mug, and sets it down, *clunk.* "'Look on my works, ye mighty, and despair.' Did you ever hear that one?"

"No!"

"I found it in one of Lance's old school books once and copied it down. Made me think of Dad, for some reason."

Dad. Mr. Vernon. "Hey, I'm—I'm sorry about him."

"You are, huh?"

"Yeah. I really am. I cried like hell when I found out."

"How'd you find out?"

"Newspaper." I don't say anything about rifling through her father's desk.

"Newspaper didn't say shit about what really happened."

"I know." I pick up my mug. The coffee's bitter, like road-tar wash-off. "Listen, Laurie—how've you been? I missed you a lot. You and Dolores and the old man. I thought about you all these years."

"Did you?"

"Oh, yeah! And the stuff we used to do. The fields, the barns, the animals! When I first came up here, I was scared of the cows, they were so big. But once your dad gave me that calf, I liked them. I used to stroke them like pets."

"Pets." She snorts. "You were a city slicker, all right. Here, you want some of this?"

She lifts a bottle of bourbon onto the bar, pours some into my coffee mug, tops up her own. Her voice is a little slurred, maybe she's been hitting the booze all evening. I hope she doesn't sit here in this empty hotel every night drinking by herself. I worry about starting on alcohol again, myself. But how can I refuse a drink with Laurie? I raise my mug so we can clink them together. She doesn't raise hers. So I just take a sip, then a longer drink. Bourbon improves the coffee's flavor a lot. It also makes my stomach queasy as hell.

"You used to like reefer," I said.

"Yeah, well...you cured me of that."

Suddenly one of the lamps in the row behind the bar blinks, blinks, goes out. Now I notice empty chairs, they look disoriented, facing in different directions. I keep peering around.

"You're looking for Dolores, aren't you?" Laurie's voice catches in her throat.

"I must be." My heart's slamming. "Yeah, I am...."

"She's gone, Pete. She's long gone."

"Aw, *hell!* How long? How long's she been gone?"

"Eleven years."

"Oh, no...." I turn away, blinking hard to keep the tears from flooding over. *Dolores!*

"What's your problem?" Laurie's glowering at me.

I wipe my cheeks against the shoulder of my t-shirt. I can't get out any words.

"You had a thing for Dolores, didn't you?"

"Sort of, sure." I try to laugh. It comes out sounding like a cough.

"There were times she was ready to jump you, too. You weren't too dumb to notice that, were you?"

My face burns.

"Yeah, you more than noticed. I knew under that sheep's clothing was a horny toad."

"It was just the one time."

She shrugs. "Sometimes I sort of hoped it'd happen."

"You did? *Why?*"

She takes a gulp from her mug and glances away. "I wasn't worrying about you and her getting serious or anything."

"We couldn't have! It—it could've ruined everything."

She cuts her eyes at me.

"I loved the farm too much. And her and you and your dad."

Laurie presses her fist against her chest. "God, I wish you hadn't!"

14

Sucker-punch! The stool wobbles beneath me.

"What the hell brought you back here, Pete?"

"I needed to see you all. One more time," I stammer.

"Why?"

"I just told you. You were important." I hold the mug tight, warm against my palm. "Important things happened here. I had to--I don't know--just *be* here again. Like, if I couldn't be sure this place existed, I wasn't sure I did. Crazy, huh?"

Laurie sighed. "I know what you mean."

"It was like that for you, too—coming back?"

Silence. She looks up at me and nods.

I loosen my grip on the mug. "Anyway, I was on my way north, I just wanted to stop for the day—"

"But you've been living here for more than four weeks."

"Yeah, well, I found your house...." I glance into the mirror. Her shoulders are rounder, so's her butt. The weight suits her. I miss that long yellow braid, though. I used to picture Dolores pulling it slowly like a bell-cord and hearing Laurie's brass tone ring over the fields. In that mirror I'm not scrawny the way I was, but my nose is still beaky and my cheeks too sharp—still a jumpy kid in too-tight skin.

"You were on your way north—where?" Laurie asks.

"Montreal. I was going to start over there…."

She pours more bourbon into her mug, raises it to her lips, never taking her eyes off me. She looks as sad as when we were talking about Dolores. I reach into my back pocket and pull out Dolores's little tin bird with the chain dangling from it, and hold it out to her.

She leans closer. "Where'd you find this?"

"In the house. Under the roll-top desk—"

"I thought I cleaned out everything…." She holds the bird up at eye level. "What's the chain? I don't remember it."

"I put it on—"

Laurie grabs it both hands, snaps it apart. The bird pings onto the bar. Both our hands dart out to catch it. Hers slaps down first, our fingers brushing. She picks it up, slips it down her shirt inside the *serape.*

"I wanted you to have Dolores's bird," I say. "Is she…okay?"

"Wish I knew…." Laurie presses her lips together. She looks me over, at my shoulders, my arms in my tight t-shirt. "Where'd you bulk up so much? Only guys I ever saw with muscles like yours, they worked out with state equipment. You been inside again, Pete?"

"Yeah." My voice goes low. "It hasn't been all that great, since I left here."

"You can say that again!" For the first time, she flashes me a smile, but it's not a happy one. "You had to go to 'Nam, didn't you? Like my all-American brother."

"I went. How'd you know?"

"You were running your mouth to Billy—did you forget?"

"Yeah, I did." Gradually my fingers uncurl at my sides. I listen to the rain, a soft rhythm I'm beginning to like. "What did you do, Laurie? You been a girl scout all this time?"

She shakes her head very slowly. "I'm all out of cookies, Pete."

"But I heard you inherited a lot of land."

"Billy must've told you that. Did he tell you I sold most of it, bought this beautiful old dump? And hardly anybody's willing to work here? No contractor in the county's taken a bid from me."

"How come?"

"At my dad's funeral, I had a few too many, and told off some local folks. All those years ago! But this is the little town where nobody forgets. It wasn't just that, though. I was the hippie dyke peacenik—and flaunting it…." She rakes her fingers back through her spikey hair. "You know, I came back here just a while before you did, isn't that something? Had big, big plans. I was going to fix up this place real nice again, bring back the family name!"

"Sounds good to me."

"Another dream—like the music. You probably heard about that, didn't you?"

"I guess it didn't work out. That's all I heard."

"Okay. I just want to know what you know," she says. "And to find out…what I might be up against tonight."

"Up against?"

She shifts her weight, not all that steady on her feet. "You're not thinking about some kind of *hostage situation* here, are you?"

"What?" I squint at her. "Laurie—what the fuck are you talking about?"

From under the counter she pulls out a rifle, rests it across one bent arm. It's the gun that used to hang in the office at her house! "Just in case you got something…dramatic on your mind," she says. "I'm still a good shot, Pete. I grew up shooting ticks off a deer's ass with a .22."

She starts to lean the gun up at an angle on the shelf behind the bar. It slips, the barrel cracks against the globe of a lamp. Flakes of frosted glass tinkle to the floor. Another bulb binks out. The lit area around us is smaller now, like we're huddled together inside a luminous tent with the dark night outside. She slowly lies the gun in the space between the busted lamp and the mirror.

"Listen, I'd never hurt you," I say. "You can put that away."

"It's been a long time, Pete. I've been living here alone, and it gets goddamn spooky sometimes. Last time I knew you, you were a teenage felon. Then your crazy, frantic letter comes. And I've been hearing strange stuff about you."

"From that sheriff you got trailing me?"

"Deputy." Laurie shrugs. "The town can't afford a sheriff."

"What's he doing, coming after me?"

"He took the surveillance job on his own. But he couldn't keep up with a three-legged armadillo. Folks only elected him 'cause everybody knows how much he likes to cruise around in that long boat of his. Still loves to listen in on police radio bands from all over the state."

"Is the radio saying anything about me these days?"

"Search me. He won't talk to 'civilians' about 'top secret' stuff." Laurie shrugs. "He's 79 years old. But you know what? He's one of the few friends I've got now. We go way back. He was the first cop that ever busted me. I was 16, D and D at a gin-mill on Route 145. The state troopers tried to put cuffs on me—I'd kicked one of them in the nuts—but he wouldn't let 'em do it."

"No shit?"

"Yep. Anyway, a few weeks ago he drove by my house and spotted you coming out of the pond. Said you looked like a rough customer."

"Guess his eyesight's okay."

"Sure…but now that you're right here in front of me, you don't look much like the desperado he was talking about. You seem like the kid that just got back from the barn."

"I know." I grin. "It's sort of like I just left your place half a minute ago, in the middle of saying something—and now I'm stepping back again to finish the sentence--"

"To finish…*what?*" Her voice is a whip-snap, and anything like a smile has vanished from her face. "I can't believe you come to town, crash in my house, start cleaning and painting and cutting the grass—then just drop by here to say 'Hi!'"

"Well…I been worrying about something for a long time…."

"Yeah?" She drums her fingers on the bar.

"Listen, you remember when—eleven years ago— when all hell broke loose at the camp?"

"Forget? Are you kidding? That changed *everything!*"

"I know it did—" I pull my cigarettes out of my jeans and raise them in her direction. She shakes her head. My fingers are trembling so hard it takes me three matches to get a smoke lit. "Okay, what it is…I was worrying you might have thought I was in on the raid. When that guy Wayne and his friend stole the plants from your garden."

"*Were* you in on it?"

"*No!* I wasn't anywhere near your place that night!"

She plants her fists on her hips. "And that's what you come to tell me, after all this time?"

"Partly." She has to be glad to hear right from my mouth that I didn't steal from her garden, doesn't she? "I never saw you—to tell you—after the raid and the riot. It made me crazy, what you might have thought about me!"

"And here you are. Well, Pete, I was pretty sure you never came rabbiting into my garden that night, yourself." She chuckles, and I'm so relieved, I feel like laughing or dancing. I picture Laurie and me dancing around this big old dining room, just the two of us with the rain sliding down the windows, we're whirling and laughing at how dizzy we are.

But she's still cutting her eyes at me. "That Wayne kid testified at the hearing," she says, "that it was only him and the Puerto Rican boy who ripped off the plants and carried them back to the camp."

"That's right!" I drain my mug. "Wait—what *hearing?* I thought Wayne and Rincon just got transferred to another joint, and that was it."

"They weren't being tried. Dolores and me—*we* were on trial."

"You? Hey, I didn't know that! Just for growing the plants?"

121

"Local DA wanted to run for state legislature, make a name for himself. It was a bullshit deal, start to finish."

"So you didn't…do time, or anything."

"Nah. We paid a hundred bucks, misdemeanor. But that wasn't the problem. That's not why you've stuck in my craw like gristle all these years."

My heart thuds hard. *"Why?"*

"Okay, Pete—here's your big chance! You got to have more on your mind you need to dump on me. Go ahead!" She steps closer to the rifle, rests her arm along the shelf below its stock. "You want to come clean? Then tell me what happened that night—while your buddy Wayne was rampaging through my garden by the light of the moon!"

"Shit, he wasn't my buddy! I hated Wayne."

"But it *was* you that told him about the garden, wasn't it?"

Her stare burns. I drop my face. "Yeah, it was me. But listen, I didn't give him any directions. He had an old map. I was sure he'd get lost in the dark, or get picked up by the state troopers. Or you'd open fire with the gun and scare him away!"

"Dolores and me were out playing a gig that night."

"I didn't know that."

"Afterwards, I figured you had to be the one who blabbed about our garden. It was a rotten thing to do. But hell, you were only fifteen." She picks up the bottle, pours some more bourbon into her mug, then mine. "How about you keep talking, Slick. You remember I used to call you that? You liked it. So tell me how slick you were that night!"

"Well…Wayne brought back the plants and everybody went crazy." I grip the mug tight. "But it wasn't some big, happy party, if you're thinking that. What they did--it was the worst goddamn thing that ever happened to me!"

"I heard about a…gang-bang."

I'm getting dizzy and I suddenly need to puke, but I clamp my teeth until it passes. "You—you heard about that?"

"Yeah. I heard that nobody would say anything about it for sure. You, especially."

"If I'd told, I'd have been dead meat," I whisper. I think, That might have been better.

"But my father knew. The troopers told him how they found you bleeding with your pants down to your ankles. He couldn't stand thinking something like that had happened to you, and on his watch."

I drag hard on my cigarette, keeping as steady as I can.

"The troopers took Dad to the camp office that night and grilled him about the riot," Laurie says. "Bastards made him think he should've stopped it all single-handed. They yelled at him, shoved him up against the filing cabinets. He had a mean bruise on his forehead…." She wipes her eyes. "He already blamed himself for what had happened to you. He was that way."

"It wasn't his fault!"

"*I* know that. But what I never could find out was how the whole damn thing could have got started, when you *knew* in advance that your buddy'd escaped the place." Laurie bangs her fist on the counter. "What happened in the barracks, Pete? *Before* all hell broke loose? While my father was talking to you? Didn't you say *anything* to him?"

My gut's turning over. It's not just the awful coffee and bourbon that's making me queasy. I remember Mr. Vernon, the shadowy barracks, the line of dim rodent eyes glowing along the ceiling.

That night, I tell Laurie, I couldn't sleep for worrying about what Wayne would do. I knew he'd jimmied open the barracks window and left the camp grounds through a secret hole under the fence, but I told myself over and over that he and Rincon would get lost, or give up the idea of a raid, or start hitch-hiking downstate and out of my life.

"I wanted to tell Mr. Vernon about Wayne being gone, but I kept hoping I wouldn't have to," I say. "See, I knew Wayne had told other kids he was going, and these kids would nail me as a snitch if I opened my mouth. I'd seen what happened to snitches."

"Yeah...."

"At the end of the barracks were these two ratty old armchairs. The old man sat in one when he wasn't doing bunk-checks. That night, he let me sit up in the chair facing him, like he always did when I couldn't asleep. He told me stories about his life on the farm. He liked to talk about his son, Lance. Like he was a kind of hero."

"That was my brother, all right—according to Dad. I could never measure up...." Laurie glares out the window. Headlights sweep by, explode silently against the mirror like camera flashes, and a boat-shaped silhouette vanishes into the rain. "Go on!" she says.

"He talked kind of slow that night. 'When my boy Lance was about your age,' he said, 'he broke into a house, took some money.' As I listened to this, I felt bad—almost *betrayed* that Lance had done something like that. But also I was relieved. Because Lance was sounding like a guy like me—just a kid who'd got in trouble. And that hadn't kept Mr. Vernon from still loving him."

Laurie leans over the bar. "Give me one of your cigarettes."

I shake one out of the pack. She takes it and I light it.

"Your dad went on—'Sheriff phoned me around midnight. Lance had got himself drunk in some gin-mill, bragging about the money he'd took. Next morning, the judge let him off. It was the first offence, and the man knew how bad we needed Lance around the farm. He was a real good worker. Didn't mind plowing til way after sundown. He said he could see furrows in the moonlight.'"

Laurie taps her cigarette on a glass ashtray she's clunked down.

"A crooked smile cracked open on the old man's face. He said, 'I don't care what anybody thought—Lance weren't a bad boy at all!'" I like talking slow like the old man, it sort of brings him back to life.

"He did plow after dark," Laurie says, her voice quiet. "I never knew how he did it. The tractor lights weren't that strong. One night, when I was little, Lance brought me back a hurt raccoon baby he'd found in the dark. It's eyes had lit up in the beams. He helped me build a house for it beside the porch."

"I didn't know that." I clear my throat. "So, anyway...the barracks were quieter than I'd ever heard them. Then Mr. Vernon said, 'After Lance's fourth robbery—he stole a car, just to ride around in, to show off—the judge told him he'd give him a choice. A last chance. He could go to reform school...or join the army.'"

"*Goddammit!* Dad never told me about that deal! I always thought poor patriotic Lance joined the service to live up to what my old man wanted!" Laurie bites her lip. "All right, what'd my father say then?"

"He said... 'I thought what the judge offered was a good deal—I was *grateful* to him.'"

Laurie shakes her head slowly. "Grateful...."

"But Lance didn't like it. He said he might take two or three years to get out of the military, but he could finish with reform school in a few months. So he'd take reform school.' Mr. Vernon sighed hard. Then he said, 'But I talked him out of that.'"

"Oh, *shit!*"

I feel more queasy. "The old man asked me, 'Why'd I talk my boy out of reform school? *Why?*' His voice was wobbly. 'It was because I was ashamed,' he said. 'Of my own son!'"

"*Ashamed?*"

"Your dad said, 'If Lance had gone to reform school, everyone in town would know he was a jailbird! I couldn't abide the shame of it.' Then I asked, 'So he joined the army?' Mr. Vernon's mouth twisted into a smile. 'Yes, sir. Lance enlisted in the infantry. I was proud of him. I'm a vet, myself.'"

"The old bastard!" Laurie's fist hits the bar. "He never said *any* of this to me!"

"He told me something else," I go on. "He said, 'You know, the night before Lance was going to ship out overseas, he got awful drunk. He come stumbling home. He said he'd changed his mind, didn't want to go into the service after all. Those Congs over there, they never done nothing to me! he said. He was just drunk, just young, you know.' And I said, 'Yeah.' Because I knew about

126

being just drunk, just young. The old man said, 'But I got real mad at Lance. So mad I smacked him in the jaw. I didn't mean to *hurt* him! I just meant to knock some sense—'"

"'Knock some sense!' How many times did I hear *that?*"

"Mr. Vernon dropped his chin to his chest. He whispered, 'I didn't know then….' He couldn't talk for a few seconds. The smoke rose up from his pipe bowl like his fist was squeezing it out. 'I didn't know then that I wasn't going to see Lance again.' I asked, 'Never?' He shook his head. His eyes shone all wet. 'Lance never come back from Vietnam alive.'"

"He never did," Laurie whispers.

"Mr. Vernon said, 'You know, Pete, If I hadn't hit him, he might not of shipped out. He might of just gone to a place like…well, like this camp, instead. And he'd be alive today!'"

"Oh, Dad…."

I listen to her breaths until they slow a little. Then I go on. "I asked him, 'Hey, are you okay?' He blinked hard and got to his feet. 'Reason I love this job so much,' he said, 'I can make sure the kids here are safe. Kids like you. If I didn't have this job, after what happened to Lance, I don't think I could stand to keep going….'"

Laurie nods. "I heard him say that, too."

"Then he said, 'I got to make the rounds. You go to sleep, Pete.' I pictured the old man shuffling up the corridor, checking each kid in his bunk. Top bunk, lower bunk—that was his routine. Then he'd come back and sit down in his chair and stare the length of the room for another hour, all alone. 'I'm not sleepy,' I said. 'Go on, now,' he said. 'You got to chop down trees tomorrow.' I told him, 'That's okay. I'll wait here for you.' He took a few steps toward the bunks. I heard his work boots scraping against the floor. Then he stopped and turned to me...."

"Yeah?" Laurie cocks her head.

"I never forgot this. He turned and said, 'You ain't a bad boy at all, Pete.'"

Laurie's still staring at me.

"Everything started to change then," I said.

"What'd you do?"

"That's when...I told him." My stomach lurches again.

"Told him *what?*" Laurie reaches behind her for the rifle. The barrel rattles the lamp fixture. "This damn well better be good, Slick!" she says. "Because I'm about ready to blow somebody's head off!"

15

I walk toward the far end of the room, holding my stomach. Car tires shish past the window on the wet road. I get an impulse—and see myself running straight out the door, a car's steel impact exploding me into the darkness, into the...*nothing*—

"Were the hell're you going?" Laurie calls.

Her voice has a frayed edge to it that I don't remember ever hearing. I don't answer, just need to move, shake off the nausea.

"You show up here, tell me all this stuff...." She's pacing in back of the bar, her boots echoing. "But *I* come back, wander around town like a ghost. Most people pretend they don't see me. They think *I* got the camp closed down, killed the golden goose. *I'm* the one that lost everybody their cushy state jobs all those years ago. So I hole up in this hotel by myself for weeks and weeks, all alone, going half crazy...." She stops moving. The room goes quiet. "Now you're going to leave me dangling in the goddamn wind—"

I hold a chair back to steady myself, turn toward her.

"So that night," she goes on, "you repaid my old man for all he did for you—by keeping your mouth shut about the raid?"

"I did at first. I was scared…."

Her arm cocks back. She flings her mug at me. It flies past my ear, shatters a window behind me. *"That's what you came back to confess? Now you think you're off the hook? And you can go on your way to—to wherever you're going to start* over?*"*

"No—"

"You didn't tell me what you said to my dad!"

"Okay…." I walk slowly back to the bar. "After he told me the story about Lance…I showed him the wrapped-up dummy Wayne had stuffed in his bunk. I told him where Wayne had gone. And how he was going to come back from your place and sell the plants in the barracks."

"A little late, weren't you? *You damn little chickenshit?*"

"I know what I was then, Laurie! But after your father told me about Lance, I couldn't keep quiet—any longer—" I press my hand over my mouth. My breath has turned to awful gulps, the start of puking.

"What's the matter with you?"

I spot a male stick-figure sign on a door at the end of the bar and lurch off toward it. Inside, I crash into a stall, skid to my knees. The revolting bourbon and coffee stream up my throat, surge after surge. They finally stop, but I keep heaving and gagging. As hard as I try to turn myself inside out, I can't get free of whatever's still deep down in my gut.

The dining room seems smaller as I shuffle back across it. Hard to imagine it packed with long-haired guys and girls in flowered dresses listening to Laurie and Dolores belting out "Me and Bobby Mcgee." The lamps just below the long mirror blur into splotches of light. On the windows they're reflected dim as candles. My mouth tastes rancid. The scent of the rain through the broken window is stronger, but I smell something else, too, something gritty.

"Laurie?" My voice echoes against the high walls. *"Laurie!"*

No answer. I can feel her absence. But it's not silent in here. A new sound fills the place—the rumble of an idling car engine, parked very near. A stink of exhaust fumes hangs in the air. Headlight beams shoot into the room. I squint through the glass, goose-bumps on my skin. A car faces the window nearest the door—a burly animal with arrogant screaming eyes that glow like they got the right to glare in and scorch me. On top, a blue flasher bar's gleaming. Not flashing, just…awake. Waiting. It's a city squad car. Has somebody—Laurie or the deputy—called it?

I don't want this. *I can't take prison again!* I've said it ever since my last discharge—*I can't go back in!* I'm bulked up, sure, but I'll get sent to a max joint this time, where guys will be in gangs, and I'll be some con's bitch or get beaten to a pulp in my cell, crippled and drooling for the rest of my miserable life. I'll never go back! *I'd rather be dead!* That's the cold truth, I mean it.

I squint at the bar. The rifle's gone. Goddamn it, Laurie's got it and she's gone off somewhere—

I hear clumping footsteps overhead. She must be pacing up there. I rush around the room looking for doorways that might lead to stairs. Now I see an eerie glint from a corner—a doorway I hadn't noticed before. It seems to have just opened in the wall this second, all aglow. I race through it.

I'm in the hotel's lobby. A boarded-up front door, a wide desk with empty cubby-holes behind it, some sofas—all lit by a few bulbs in a mostly naked chandelier that hangs above a staircase with a curved railing. I rush up the steps. At the top, I run into a long white hallway and stop, wheezing for breath.

The ceilings show jagged cracks like strokes of horizontal lightening. Around a corner, the hallway's lit by upside-down mushroom-shaped bulbs. They grow dimmer as I walk deeper into the building. I seem to be walking back through my life. Maybe this really was the resort my mother visited before I was born, the place where she bought the birch-bark canoe. Somewhere there could be verandahs, decks overlooking a mill stream….

Up here, shadowy tunnels lead off in different directions. More footsteps. I stop, listen. Laurie's footsteps stop, too—like she's fallen off the end of a landing and left me alone in the huge building. But I feel the echo of a movement in the air--she's been here seconds ago. Ahead of me, up a dark corridor, an ajar doorway spills a sliver of light onto the floor.

"Laurie?"

A sigh of cloth. Sounds are magnified in this hall. The room's breathing. I walk toward the light, shielding my eyes with my hand…push open the door.

Laurie's sitting on a bed against the room's far wall. Windows gleam like tall slabs of black marble. A lot of other people, larger than life, are here, too—singers and musicians staring down from wall posters. Soulful eyes, ecstatic grins, stoned blue gazes. As soon as I start gazing back, my eyes swirl, I'm swerving the outlines of bright, psychedelic designs. A woman's hair flows along curlicues of a word whose letters billow like wind-bloated sails. Figures brandish guitars that shoot showers of silver notes. There's crazy-eyed Janice Joplin, who sang "Bobbie Mcgee." And Joan Baez with the long dark hair, Dolores's poster for an all-Spanish album, *"Gracias a la Vida."* And there's Dolores and Laurie with their guitars, their beautiful smiles—dozens of pictures and yellowed newspaper clippings of them tacked to the crumbling plaster walls.

Flesh-and-blood Laurie, in her jeans and shit-kicker boots and *serape*, sits on the bed glaring up at me.

She's holding the rifle across her knee.

"Hello, Slick," she says. The gun's barrel turns slowly. The muzzle points at my chest. "Aren't you glad you found me today."

The air's stale, dusty, hard to inhale. I'm in another land, a place deep inside another time. "Yeah, I'm glad, Laurie." She looks younger now. I seem younger, too. I even feel like kidding around with her again, even though she's glowering at me like I'm the devil's spawn.

"You want me to put my hands up in the air or something?" I ask.

I see a glitter in her eye, smell her bourbon breath. "Do what the hell you want," she says. That brassy voice again, the one I love. "I just figured out what I can do with you to save my sorry ass."

"You ass looks okay."

"Shut up, Slick! You're *my hostage* now!" She grins. "You're an outlaw I've captured, a criminal on the lam who's come in here to threaten me. But I talked you into giving up your weapon—" She pats the top of the gun barrel, returns her hand to the trigger. "And now I'm turning you over to the law."

"You *did* call the cops on me!"

"I didn't call anybody, Pete. I just saw that cruiser pull up out front. I 'spect the police caught up with you from New York City or wherever you were. Maybe the deputy picked up a signal on the scanner and contacted them, said you were headed to the hotel." She shrugged. "Anyway, that city cop's going to do me a favor now."

"Would you turn me in?"

"What do you think?"

The posters throb at me from the walls. I take a deep breath. "No. You wouldn't, Laurie."

"What makes you so certain? What makes you so goddamn sure of yourself, after everything that's happened?"

"Shit, I don't know. Nothing left to lose, I guess. You remember that song?"

"Shut up, dammit! I'm serious!"

I nod. "Me, too."

"I've been thinking hard about doing this since I saw that patrol car."

"Well, don't think about it. I won't let you turn me in!"

She watches me for some long seconds. "I *should* turn you in!"

"Sounds like a great song. Did you just write it?"

"Yep."

"How's the melody go?"

"I'm working on it."

"Okay. I'll have to wait, then." I spot a fat armchair in a corner. In two steps, I've flopped down into it, my hands hanging over the sides, my head lolling back. "Be careful with that gun. If you blow my brains out, it'll make a hell of a mess on this nice chair."

"*You* be careful," she says.

"It's your fucking chair."

"Don't you care about your brains?"

"No big loss. I haven't used them for much lately."

She scrambles up off the bed, gripping the rifle in one hand. "You think this is some big joke, some caper of yours! But I wouldn't *mind* shooting you!"

I stand up, too. "Go ahead, Laurie. Do it!"

"You're a goddamn screwball, Slick!"

"Takes one to know one."

She steps unsteadily toward me, the barrel waving in the air. "You know, my dad couldn't stand being fired from that job he loved! He thought he'd let all the boys down, losing control of the barracks that night. He felt like he'd let *you* down, Pete!"

"He never did—"

"It broke his heart!" Her eyes are shiny. "I mean, it literally—*broke—his—heart!*"

All my jokiness has drained out of me. "I know."

"Everything was over, after that riot. I lost my dad. And then Dolores!"

I blink hard. Laurie's blurred, blended into the pictures. "Why—why'd you lose her?"

"After our hearing, that hotshot DA got her extradited to Texas because her papers weren't legal. Then the cops there sent her back to Mexico." Laurie stares down at the floor. "I went down there, trying to bring her back, but I couldn't find a lawyer where she was living. People in her village were suspicious of me. Her family was after her to take a maid's job for a rich local family, so she could support them…."

"Damn!"

"I had to go home without her. I wrote her. But over the years, we just…lost touch."

I know she's picturing Dolores. Her longing heats up my own memories of her, like she's blowing on hot coals. I must be making hers more painful, too. Yet we keep our stares fastened on each other because there's a comfort in sharing them that we can't afford to let go of.

"I don't even know where she *is* any more!" Laurie says.

"I'm sorry," I say. And I really am.

But it doesn't stop me from jumping forward and wrenching the rifle out of her hand. I hold it high in the air in one hand.

"Hey!" She lunges for it, face burning, fingers like claws on my arm. *"You bastard!"* Her forehead butts against my jaw but I keep the rifle out of her reach. "Why'd you have show up here? Make me think about everything all over again?"

"You know why!"

"What're you going to do now? Just run off again?"

"Not very far. Only as far as I need…to go." I turn toward the sound of the cruiser growling downstairs. Then I look around at the walls, at photos of her and Dolores and all their poster friends. "You better stay upstairs here."

"Why? What's going to happen?"

"You don't want to be in the way of it." I try to wrench my arm out of her grip. "You could get hurt."

"What the hell d'you mean?"

"You can live to tell the tale, Laurie." I grab her shoulder, ready to push her off. "You can live to sing your song."

16

We're a hell of a dance team, me and Laurie! I'm charging down the hallways, the rifle held above my head. She's lurching along with me as she grabs for it, her arm half-wrapped around my shoulder. Her legs tangle with mine, we keep crashing against walls. I don't know where the fuck I'm going in this maze of shadows.

We bump together at a dead end. She hammers me with her fists. I break free. She gets in a solid whack to my cheek. Salty blood clogs my throat. I've only got one hand free, she's got two. I'm tempted to slam her head with the stock of the gun, but I couldn't stand doing that. She grabs my hair in her fist—*ow, shit!*—cracks my head against the wall. Reeling, I clip her with the back of my hand, split her lip. Her face flames up red—

"I told you—*get back!*" I scream. "Fucking *bitch*—let go!"

She kicks my ankle hard. "*You crazy bastard*—give me that thing!"

Limping with pain, I break into a run. She's after me again, grabbing at my shirt from behind. I lunge out onto a landing above a flight of stairs. My palm squeaks on a railing. I stumble to the bottom into the hotel lobby, swerve off through the door into the dining room.

It's flooded with headlight glare, I have to shield my eyes with my hand to see anything. The car's flasher bar starts spurting blue light against the windows. I know it's Rand, himself, out there. He's watching me through his windshield. His pistol's probably resting on the seat next to him, safety off. He used to brag about his sharpshooting scores. One quick burst should do it.

Laurie staggers up behind me. The engine growls louder. If I knew for sure I'd be the only one to get hit, I'd go crashing out the door right now, blasting away at the sky to draw fire. Blue light flickers over Laurie's face like splashes of paint. Down on one knee, I raise the gun to my shoulder and sight along the barrel at her.

"What're you—*doing?*" She screams. But she stops where she is.

It's for show, for the cop outside. I face the door. *"Turn off your damn lights!"* My voice is amplified by the walls. *"Get back!"*

Rand must hear me. The blue stops flashing, the beams die. Only an angled spotlight streaks through a window at the far end of the room. A lull. He's going to wait me out for a while.

"What are you thinking about doing?" Laurie sways in place, wiping blood from her lip.

"Get behind the bar!" I wave the gun barrel toward it.

"That cop must have a high-powered rifle! You'll get killed! Is that what you want?" She waits for an answer.

I swallow hard, choking on my spit.

She steps toward me. "Pete, you don't need to do this."

"Go on, Laurie!" I gesture toward the bar again. What she said about *high powered rifle* is making me jumpy. "The last thing I want," I croak, "is your getting hit when it starts."

"Christ almighty, what'd you *do* to get the law after you like this?"

I shake my head hard. "Listen, Laurie—I'm never going back to prison."

"What the hell did you *do?*" The spotlight beam flashes off the mirror, keeps Laurie's face lit up, bruised and splotched, her cut lip shiny red.

Finally I sit down on one of the stray chairs, the rifle across my knee. "I took some money. It was crazy. I took it from a cop—the one outside. A stupid impulse—a kind of pay-back—"

"*Why, Pete?*" She looks like she wants to punch me again, but much harder.

I tell her about not being able to help Raquel, and her overdose death in my apartment. I tell her about breaking open Lieutenant Rand's locker, exploding the bag of coke against the wall, grabbing up his stash of bills in a panic. I keep glancing outside every few seconds. Rand's switched on the flasher bar again, playing freak-out games. The rain out there looks like silent fireworks exploding in a blue fogbank. Then the noise again--the engine revving and rattling the room's windows. It's a funhouse of the damned in here.

I point the rifle at the door.

Laurie lunges, knocks the muzzle sideways. *"Don't! He'll shoot back!"*

Not with her hanging onto me like this. The spotlight beam flashes through the room, streak across the wall. "Why don't you back off from me, Laurie?" I yank the gun free. "I'm a lost cause."

"What d'you think *I* am? I can't even turn in a dangerous outlaw and clear my name in this town." She laughs out of the side of her mouth. "Damn, Pete—you don't have to blame yourself for what happened to your girlfriend. Any more than you do for my father!"

"I told you how I let him down in the barracks."

She pulls a chair over and sits down, breathing hard. "Well, *I* didn't tell you everything."

"What do you mean?"

"Okay, Listen. After you told my dad about the raid...do you remember what he did?"

"He said to get in my bunk and keep quiet. He got his keys out and headed for the far end of the room. There was a locked box on the wall by the door there. It had an emergency phone inside."

"Did you see him unlock it?"

"I couldn't see much from my bunk."

"Well, from what he said to me, it was the barracks door he unlocked, not the phone box. He went outdoors and sat in his truck. He had a pint bottle he kept in the glove compartment."

"He didn't phone?"

"He couldn't make up his mind what to do. If he called the troopers, they might pick up the boys on the road, then he'd get blamed for letting them escape. And he might lose his job. The last kids who ran away got scared in the woods and came back on their own. So he was hoping that'd happen again."

"Yeah...but if I'd told him earlier, he might have called the troopers then, instead of when it was too late. They might have caught Wayne—"

"That's what I was thinking before." Laurie stares down. "If my dad had had more time, he'd've done the right thing!"

"He would have! He always did the right thing!"

"I wanted to think so, too. All the time I was growing up. He was usually so good to us!" Laurie's eyes go damp. "But the goddamn truth was, he had his real bad spells. We paid for them, my mom and me, and Lance, too."

"But—"

"*But—hell!* We got to face it, Pete! He might've sat in that damn truck drinking and fidgeting til dawn!"

"Maybe…."

"I didn't want to see what he was like in those days. I was keeping busy with Dolores and my music. We were getting good! We were planning to go on the road, lining up gigs—"

"You were going to leave Oak Hollow?"

"Yeah. And I think my dad knew it. Though I hadn't worked up to telling him yet. I could see he was drinking more. The anniversary of Lance's death was coming." Laurie blinks hard. "I wasn't around as much as I should've been…to spend time with him."

"Maybe that's why he told me about Lance and the judge—"

"He should've told *me!*" Laurie jumps to her feet, her eyes flashing in the harsh light. "I was his *daughter!* Who the hell were *you?*"

17

Outside the windows, I see the cruiser's door open a crack.
The dim interior light outlines Rand's shoulders and bullet
head, his features dissolved in shadow. Something flicks in
front of his face. A rifle. He's positioning it to shoot from
behind the car door, using the top hinge for a mount.
Crackly static—a police radio. He jerks to snap it off,
turns back toward the hotel door. The blue light flashes
faster.

Going down in flames—or in a barrage of bullets—
that's always had a logic for me. An inevitability—a *lure*,
even. Now that it's about to happen, though, I'm scared
shitless and I want to hang on here a while longer. I just
found Laurie, goddammit!

She's staring hard at me as I follow the movements outside
the door. Hunkered down—ready to spring for the rifle
again? No, she looks too tired, her forehead tight with
lines. She sucks at the sore place on her lip.

"You got to step back, Laurie," I say.

"The hell I do!" Nothing wrong with that brassy
voice.

143

My eyes are blurring over trying to squint into the light.

"Pete, it was me that planted the weed in the garden. And *told* you about it. What a dumb thing to do!" She gives a hard little laugh. "Maybe I wanted to impress you about how cool I was. Like I used to impress my brother what a bad-ass sister he had—him, the big straight arrow! I wanted to get back at my old man, too. Raise the stuff right under his nose...."

"But you used to say lots of people grew it around here, it was no big deal."

"To him it was." She cocks her head. "You're trying to help me off the hook, Pete, aren't you?"

"You didn't mean to hurt your dad, Laurie—"

"When you say something like that, I remember why I liked you so much."

It's strange to hear Laurie's voice so low now, almost soft. The floor reverberates under my feet, echoes the car's engine. Suddenly the loud robot growl of a bullhorn shoots into the room.

"*COME OUT OF THERE!*" Rand's amplified voice jolts me all over. "*RIGHT NOW!*"

"*Fuck you!*" I scream back. Though I doubt if he can hear me over the engine noise. I turn away from his car.

Laurie's hugging her arms across her chest. She stares outside, wide-eyed, then turns slowly back to me. "Jeez, Pete...."

"The bastard." I kick the floor with the toe of my boot. The motor vibrates the air, stinking it up again with fumes, but the bullhorn stays silent. I hear Laurie take some deep breaths. She's scared, now. Who wouldn't be?

"Anyway—" Laurie leans over a chair back, gripping the top bar like a roller coaster seat's rail. "Anyway...you were a fuzzy-headed kid, eager to please us," she goes on. "Like Lance used to be. The problem was, sometimes the old man sort of believed you *were* Lance."

"I know. I pretended I didn't notice, though."

"I did, too. I wanted my little brother back." Her voice cracks. *"I still do...."*

I lean over to try and see her face. A strand of hair drops over my eye, I whip it back with a head-snap. I can smell myself now. Damp, sweaty.

"After Lance was killed," she says, "my dad went off the deep end. Suicide threats, wild drunks—he was hell on wheels!" Laurie blows out a weary breath. "But once you started helping him on the farm, he calmed down so much! He changed back—I could hardly believe it. You were magic!"

"Me?" I shake my head. "I helped him with his work, but—"

"You got him to be his old self again! He started working his heart out and loving it the way he always used to. He cut way back on the booze. He stopped all his carping at Dolores and me about the 'protest music' and all that. Sometimes he even listened to us singing!"

I sigh, my mouth wanting to smile. "I remember listening to you both with your guitars. With the old man, all of us out on the porch at night, with the moths flying around the light bulb above your heads."

Laurie nods. "And when we saw how you were cheering him up, keeping him sane? Pete—we *flirted* with you, just to make sure you'd keep coming to the farm! Dolores did, especially. But it wasn't just because of my dad. We *liked* you a lot, too!"

"I kept hoping you did."

The flashing blue light's scalding my eyes. Then the metallic growl, the damn bullhorn again— *"COME OUT THAT DOOR, PETE! BEFORE I HAVE TO COME IN THERE!"*

"You don't belong in here! Fuck off!" Fat chance of that. I raise the gun barrel, just to show it—make him see what a bad idea his charging inside would be. The rifle feels heavy, awkward in my hands.

"You think he'll come in?" Laurie grips the chair back.

"No, he wouldn't risk hurting you." I snap my head in his direction. *"Stay the hell out of here!"* He won't hear, but I scream anyway. *"Get away! This is Laurie's place!"*

She seems reassured, and wipes her forehead with her sleeve. "Anyway…." She pauses to catch her breath. "I worried that you might stop coming to work if you caught on to the way the old man was using you."

I frown. "He *wasn't* using me!"

"The hell he wasn't! He worked you ragged for fifty cents an hour! We saw it, Dolores and me—but we never said a word about it to him. Or to you. We knew we should have, but…."

I'm trying to breathe normally. By now the squad car's engine noise has set off a fierce buzzing in my chest that won't stop. I stand up, muscles twitching. The gun feels leaden in my hands.

"I could see what you and Dolores were doing, Laurie. But I got a charge out of playing along with it."

"Yeah, but all those ditches the old man got you digging in the rain? The fence posts you pounded in? The mountains of cow shit you shoveled? He seemed to be *punishing* you!"

"He usually worked right alongside me."

146

"Punishing himself at the same time."

I rest one foot on an empty chair, the rifle still across my knee. And I remember the first time I hefted it in my palm, raised it to my shoulder as Mr. Vernon guided my hand. It would break his heart to see what I'm planning to do with it now. I hate what Laurie's said about him exploiting me. But now I remember working so hard on the farm that when I swung my axe in the woods the next day, my shoulder seized up, red-hot with pain. But I never slowed down, I liked being a tough bastard about it. The harder I worked, the less energy I had for thinking about old things that hurt inside so bad.

"I did wonder if it wasn't illegal," I say, "all the hours the camp was letting me stay off the grounds to be on the farm. I got to skip school classes, group therapy, lots of stuff."

"The camp director had a deal going with Dad. I heard them talking on the phone. The state needed the good will of the folks in town when it set up its penal colony in their back yard. The director knew Dad still had influence here, even when he started struggling."

I stare at the floor. "Your dad always said I was helping him get through hard times."

"I know." Laurie's mouth crack into a sad grin. "And you were."

"I didn't give a shit about getting paid. Mr. Vernon needed me at the farm and I needed to be there. It was like a…a real home. He was the first person who ever wanted to help me learn stuff!" I stand straighter. "So sure, I went along with it, being like his son."

"Okay, Slick, maybe you did." Laurie sighs. "Looks like you and I both kept my dad thinking it was okay to keep deluding himself."

"I'm not sorry."

"I guess he wasn't either. But maybe if we hadn't let him get away with it, he might not have taken the riot so hard. All the violence and what happened to you afterwards. He might still be alive."

"I don't know that. How can we know?"

She presses he knuckles against her lower lip. "We can't," she whispers, and I hear the catch in her throat. "I—I miss him, Pete!"

"Me, too."

All the metallic sounds outside seem to have faded back. The room has the same dim-gold glow I saw when I first walked in and spotted the figure behind the bar who turned into Laurie and came alive again. I want to look for the mural of shepherdesses among all the shadows, listen for the old music. I feel like they could come back—if I stare and I listen hard enough.

Laurie leans forward. I rest my free hand on her shoulder. It's damp, warm. She tilts forward til her forehead's resting against my chest. I keep holding her.

The rain washes down past the windows beside us. I listen to it smacking against the gravel outside, splashing and dancing in the puddles. Its fresh damp smell blows through the broken panes. I take long, deep breaths, almost smiling.

Then the bullhorn blasts. *"LISTEN, PETE—GET YOUR ASS OUT HERE!"*

"No—I'm not listening to you any more!" I stand glaring blindly into the cruiser's lights, feeling their hot glare against my face. *"I need my time here! You fucking wait!"*

Laurie looks at me for long seconds like she's trying to figure something out. So am I. The blue light flashes faster. I jerk my head sideways, away from the damn car.

Laurie turns, too. "Pete, that cop's money you stole out of the locker in New York--how much of it did you spend?"

"What?" I catch my breath. "None of it! I didn't *steal* it ! I just grabbed it because I was out of my mind—I was stupid with fear, with grieving—"

"All right! And you still have the money?"

"Sure, every cent. Locked in the trunk of my car." I picture the Caddie gleaming outside in the rain, clean and wet. "Hey, I got a Cadillac, Laurie. An old silver one with fins, the kind you used to like. I was looking forward to showing it to you."

"Maybe you still can." She tries to smile. "Listen, that cash? It's evidence. You've got a lot of evidence on a rogue cop! You saw the drugs in his locker. He knows you did. So he sure as hell won't want to press any charges against you in the city! He'd be scared of what you'd testify."

"That's *him,* outside—the same guy! I'm sure of it!" I glare through the windows—his head's shape still behind the car windshield, the darkened featureless face.

"Damn! Are you sure?"

"Oh, yeah."

The car's revving up its noise whenever I get a few paces from Laurie. All of a sudden, I know Laurie's right about Rand not wanting to press charges. I was so freaked out about going to prison I couldn't think straight, but now it's obvious—me getting busted and locked up aren't part of his plan. He's not here for that. He's come here to blow me away!

Just what I wanted. Except I'm not sure I do any more. Now that it could be too late.

"Haven't you got anybody—a lawyer?" Laurie asks.

"Just the fuckwit that got me sprung from jail a few years ago."

"He got you out? Why's he a fuckwit, then?"

"'Cause he got me into the counseling gig run by that thug outside!"

"So?"

"So? I couldn't help Raquel, could I? I couldn't protect her from him! Not from anything!"

"You tried, Pete! You don't deserve to get killed because you tried!" She presses her fist hard against my chest. "Maybe it's time you forgive yourself for a few things."

"Maybe…." I sigh. "But hell, is anybody going to believe what I say, with my record?"

"*I* do, Pete!" she says. "My old man would have!"

"He would have…." I see how bright her eyes are, and not just reflecting the window glare. "You never really would've turned me in, would you?"

"Of course not, you jerk!"

The room goes quiet again. More flashes explode out of the mirror at me, winking like evil lizard-eyes from the gloss of the bar's woodwork. That low rumbling noise—I feel like it's been following me all my life, an echo in the back of my head.

Finally I say, "You know what, Laurie? I don't want to let that bastard get away with what he did to Raquel."

"To you, too!"

"To me, too." My heart pumps faster. "You remember what you were telling me upstairs in your room? How if you could talk me into giving up, you could save your reputation in this town?"

Laurie grabs my arm. "I could still do that! I could tell the law I calmed you down—"

"Yeah, and then…you can say I told you how I stayed with the counseling job for two years. Took other jobs. Stayed clean.

"Okay—"

"If we can get past Rand tonight—you can testify for me!"

"And I could say we talked about you coming to work with me—to fix up this hotel, get it running again! How about that?"

Our foreheads are nearly touching. The rain seems to be flooding down just inches away from us. "I *could* help you with the hotel, Laurie!"

"I know you could. I saw what you've done to my old house."

"You saw? You've been coming around?"

"Sure. I never dreamed anyone could fix up that place like you were doing." Her voice has a laugh in it. "Watching you get stuff done every day—it's probably what kept me in this town these last weeks! You're going to have to finish that work, Pete!"

"Okay!"

"Okay."

I shift the gun around, pointing the barrel between her and the door. Rand has switched off the blue lights again. But the car's side-beam spotlight swings toward us.

"I could organize painters, carpenters for the hotel— I'm good at that. A lot of the work I could do myself—"

I tap my toe hard against the floor. "You got some money to put up for me? If I ever make it out of here, I'll be running big legal bills."

"I'll put up the money! If you don't trust me to do it, who *are* you going to trust?"

"I can't think of anybody, off-hand—"

"*Off-hand*—my ass! You're like me—you've got nobody else to trust!"

What we've been talking about—bringing back this old resort—might be a screwball idea, might not. It'd be a year of good work, probably a lot more. And I really could help Laurie run the place if—when--it opened. "What else have I got to do with my life?" I say.

"That's what I've been wondering about mine." Her fingers stay on my arm--no longer squeezing, just resting.

Beyond the door, everything's a blur. The rain splashes down the window like we're in a cavern behind a silver waterfall. Laurie moves sideways to squint through a pane.

We both see it—another car gliding up like a long boat through the fog. It stops next to the squad car. The Crown Vic.

"There's my old pal. I told you he was slow," she says.

"What the hell's he doing here?"

"Checking up on you, like I said." She stares at the window. Then a grin lights her face. "You know what, Pete? With him watching, that city cop won't dare open fire on you."

"How do you know?"

She bites her lip. She doesn't know, she just hopes. "Pete, if you don't look dangerous, if you don't come out the door blasting away with the rifle—"

"He could still open fire and say I was keeping you hostage."

"Not if I didn't look like one. If I came right along with you."

"You can't do that!"

"The hell I can't!"

"Laurie—"

"I'm going out with you!" She narrows her eyes. "Don't even think about trying to stop me!"

I take a long breath. She's got a lock on my arm now. "Okay then—listen! Here's what we can do—"

We go over a plan fast. If I make it out of here, I won't speak to Rand. I'll get right into the deputy's car with Laurie. We'll tell the man to speed away from here. Later, in court, I'll spill everything I know about the lieutenant. I'll say how Laurie and I planned a future here with the hotel.

I stare at her hard. Her eyes haven't changed, they're still ready to laugh and egg me on. The way she did as she leaned out of the cab of the flatbed truck while I was getting a good grip on a hay bale, and she yelled, *Heave it up, Pete—it's not heavy!* and I thought of that song, *He ain't heavy he's my brother!* And I grinned and tossed the big, bristly thing up, watched it skid all the way across the truck's bed to thump against the back of her cab.

Rand's engine revs, vibrates in a big wave I can feel through the glass. He's trying to panic me into bolting. I don't move. He cuts the sound off. Silence. I know his gun's aimed right at me. He's ready to fire the second I step outside if he can get a clear shot.

I walk slowly to the door with Laurie. The cruiser's blue bar throbs. I raise my rifle high over my head two-handed, a position of surrender. Laurie leans forward, twists the door knob. With the toe of my boot I push the door. It swings out into the darkness.

The air's thick with the stink of exhaust fumes, clouds of them swirling in the fog. Rain splashes softly against my face. It feels cool, clean. I tighten my hold on the rifle over my head. Laurie walks close beside me. Suddenly her fingers leave my arm.

For a second, I'm alone, a bulls-eye standing in the mud, my eyes flooded with glare.

Deep in my throat I hold my breath—wait for the explosions from the cruiser—

The rifle shifts in my grip above my head. Laurie's holding it too, with both hands. Leaning against me on tiptoe, she pushes it higher in the air.

I see the Crown Vic's back door swing wide open for us. The interior light blinks and stays bright. Laurie and I turn toward it. Her wet fingers wrap tighter around the gun's barrel, touching mine.

We run forward, letting the rifle fall to the ground. I give Laurie a push toward the car. She dives across the seat.

I'm in behind her, safe. All I hear now is the soft, steady rain on our roof.

CPSIA information can be obtained at www.ICGtesting.com
Printed in the USA
BVOW071132161012

303119BV00001B/1/P